HOT LEAD RANGE

When an undercover agent going by the name of Bob Harker arrives in Sweetwater Valley, his task is to prevent a range war developing: the ruthless Butch Collins intends to claim the entire valley by forcing out his neighbours. One such neighbour is Frank Bateman — Harker's old boss when he was a Pinkerton detective. Harker manages to infiltrate the Collins outfit but, forced to take ever greater risks, could this be his final mission?

Books by Jack Holt
in the Linford Western Library:

GUNHAWK'S REVENGE
PETTICOAT MARSHAL

JACK HOLT

HOT LEAD RANGE

Complete and Unabridged

LINFORD
Leicester

First published in Great Britain in 2006 by
Robert Hale Limited
London

First Linford Edition
published 2007
by arrangement with
Robert Hale Limited
London

British Library CIP Data

Holt, Jack
  Hot lead range.—Large print ed.—
  Linford western library
  1. Western stories
  2. Large type books
  I. Title
  823.9′2 [F]

  ISBN 978–1–84617–662–3

Published by
F. A. Thorpe (Publishing)
Anstey, Leicestershire

Set by Words & Graphics Ltd.
Anstey, Leicestershire
Printed and bound in Great Britain by
T. J. International Ltd., Padstow, Cornwall

This book is printed on acid-free paper

1

'Sling that rope!' Butch Collins, the owner of the Broken Arrow ranch ordered, 'and get this hanging over with. We've got cows to brand.'

Bob Harker, the man facing the hangman's rope, said: 'This is a lynching and plain murder.'

Collins grunted. 'You saw the signs. Trespassers will be hanged on sight, that's what they say. The noose round your neck is down to your own darn foolishness.'

'You'd hang a man for merely crossing your range?' Harker questioned.

'I'd hang a man for plucking a blade of grass, mister,' Collins replied, grimfaced. 'You see,' he added by way of explanation, 'a blade of grass in cow country is akin to a nugget of gold to a prospector. Now if you had a gold-mine you'd carefully and zealously guard it

1

from interlopers, wouldn't you? Well, that's what I'm doing.'

'I'm not from these parts,' Harker said in his defence. 'As a stranger I know nothing about boundaries or range ownership in this valley. I'm an innocent who just happened to stray.'

Butch Collins guffawed.

'Aren't any innocents round here, fella. Turn your gaze the other way for a second, and when you look back your cattle have been rustled or there's a nester setting up a homestead.'

'It's open range, I believe,' Harker said.

'Well there's nothing open about what the Broken Arrow's put its mark on,' the rancher growled bitterly. 'Now hang the bastard, Larry,' he ordered the man who had put the noose round Bob Harker's neck.

Bound as he was, there was nothing Harker could do to dissuade his lynchers.

'Mebbe we should just whup him and send him on his way, Mr Collins,' suggested an older man, who was obviously uneasy with a lynching. 'It ain't the way your pa would have done things.'

'You've never had the guts for cow country, Daly,' Collins sneered. 'My pa is dead, and things will be done my way now. And if you don't like it, you can always up roots and ride. In fact,' he growled, 'that might be a good idea. Seems to me that you've been around too long anyway, Daly.'

'Your pa told me before he died that I had a job with the Broken Arrow for as long as I wanted,' Daly said shakily.

Butch Collins lashed out at the older man, knocking him flat on his back. He thought about following through with a boot to the ribs but held back. Not because he was of a charitable frame of mind, Harker reckoned, but because of the critical witness of some of the men, long-term pards of Daly.

Not so the two men who hung back like vultures waiting for a meal. They were disappointed that Collins had drawn back from inflicting terrible injury on the man who had questioned him. The much-travelled Harker had seen men like them before — born killers from the second they left their mother's womb. Collins grabbed the noose.

'I'll hang him myself!'

Harker felt the bite of the rope round his neck as Butch Collins tightened the noose. He swept off his hat and was ready to send the horse that Harker sat astride charging off when a man's voice ordered:

'Swat that horse's hindquarters and I'll cut you down, Collins!'

Furious, Butch Collins swung around to face the man standing on the rise of ground behind him, toting a shotgun.

'The same goes for each and every man,' he warned.

'This is none of your business, Rattigan,' Butch Collins ranted. 'You're only a town star-packer. You have no say in the valley.'

'I tote a badge, Collins,' Rattigan

flung back. 'That makes illegal hangings my business in town or county,' he grated.

'I'd say that Butch has got ev'ry right to hang trespassers, Sheriff,' one of the vultures said. A lanky fleshless specimen who, were he a meal, would be a sore disappointment to the scavenger he reminded Harker of. 'He's posted fair warning on the range.'

'The last time I checked, Smallwood,' Rattigan growled, 'trespass was not a hanging offence.'

'Wouldn't you agree, Stan?' Smallwood asked the second half of the duo he formed.

'I'd say, Bengy,' Stan drawled, Texas in his voice. He shifted his stance, letting his hand drop to the butt of his sixgun.

'If you so much as flinch, Baker,' Rattigan told the man called Stan, 'you'll meet the devil sooner than you planned.'

'You have no right to threaten my men, Rattigan,' Butch Collins barked.

'In fact,' Collins grinned with sly evil, 'we'd have every right to sling another rope for you, seeing as you've ridden uninvited on to Broken Arrow range, too.'

'Try, Collins,' Rattigan growled. He levelled the shotgun on the rancher. 'Just try.'

'That's real threatening talk, Sheriff,' Stan Baker said, pushing for a confrontation.

'You read the trespass signs, didn't you, Sheriff?' Smallwood said. 'Fair warning, I'd say.'

'Mebbe the sheriff can't read, Bengy,' Baker sniggered.

Stan Baker, Harker knew by reputation. A killer who hired out his gun to the highest bidder.

'Real dumb critters, some lawmen I knowed,' Smallwood sniggered.

'I told you fellas to quit the territory,' Rattigan barked.

'Yeah,' Baker agreed. He slid back his hat and scratched his head. 'Said that you'd chase Bengy and me clear outta the territory if we didn't hightail it.'

Baker stood shoulder to shoulder with Smallwood.

'Well, we ain't done as you said, Sheriff.'

Bengy Smallwood flung out a challenge. 'Now what are you aimin' to do about that, Sheriff?'

Butch Collins's grin was as wide as the Grand Canyon.

'Now boys, don't you go scaring the sherriff like that,' he said snidely. 'He might just fall apart from shivering in his boots.'

'First things first,' Rattigan said, seemingly unshaken. 'Get that rope from around the stranger's neck,' he ordered Collins.

Bob Harker concluded that the lawman was one of two things, a very brave, fearless and just man, or the biggest fool since the start of Creation. And from his own point of view, he hoped that in the next couple of seconds Rattigan would be able to back his stand. Or they'd both be swinging in the stiffish fall breeze.

Butch Collins scoffed in open defiance of the sheriff.

'I don't think I'm of a mind to do that, Rattigan. You see, you let one trespassing bastard go, and before you know it you'll have the range full of nesters. No, sir. Lessons have to be taught and learned.'

'I'll say it one more time, Collins,' Rattigan threatened. 'Cut the stranger loose!'

Collins's response to the lawman's ultimatum was: 'Hang him!'

The two men he had addressed hesitated, their eyes flashing Rattigan's way.

'What're you waiting for?' Collins barked at the reluctant hangmen. Then, angrily: 'Damn you, ride out before I kill you both.'

The men mounted up and galloped off.

'Guess I'll have to hang this hobo myself, after all,' he said.

Bart Rattigan's Greener exploded.

The tree-branch over which the lynch-rope had been slung shattered. The horse bolted, pitching Harker to the ground.

'Give the stranger a horse,' was the sheriff's uncompromising order.

One was readily supplied by a shaking man who had narrowly escaped being crowned by the falling tree-branch.

'Be on your way,' Rattigan told Harker, the instant he was in the saddle.

'I don't reckon it's right to leave you alone with these killers, Sheriff,' Harker said. 'After you saving my neck.'

'I only did what needed doing,' the lawman bellowed impatiently. 'Now git!'

Harker spurred the horse and galloped off.

'This ain't the end of this!' Butch Collins called after Harker. Rattigan now turned his attention to Baker and Smallwood.

'Haven't you gents got some place to go?'

Baker shot Collins a glance. He

returned a neutral look, but anticipating Rattigan's stance, had arranged for the hardcases to hide out nearby.

'We're going, Sheriff,' Baker said. 'But that don't mean we ain't coming back.'

'Do, and I'll kill you,' Rattigan stated, with cold-eyed resolve.

'I'll remind you, Rattigan,' Butch Collins snarled, 'that Stan and Bengy are legitimate employees of the Broken Arrow ranch.'

'They're gun-thugs, Collins!' Rattigan barked. 'Like I said,' he turned his attention back to the hired guns, 'if I set eyes on you again, I'll kill you.'

'Who gets killed remains to be seen, lawman,' Baker said when saddled up.

'There ain't no guarantees, Rattigan,' Smallwood added.

From long experience, Bart Rattigan knew the truth of what the gunfighter said.

2

Harker rode hard and fast, easing his pace only when he was certain that he was off Broken Arrow grass. Fortunately his gallop was tailing off when, rounding a sharp bend in the narrow trail, he almost collided with a buggy hogging the middle of the road.

Harker watched in horror as the buggy veered off the trail down a steep embankment. And not only was the slope steep, but it was very uneven and covered with thick brush and spindly trees. The embankment would not be easily negotiated under the best conditions, but in a buggy that was out of control terrible disaster seemed inevitable.

He turned his horse and clipped it after the buggy, jostling with it to grab hold of its horse's reins while trying to avoid being side-swiped by either the buggy or a branch of a tree. By now the woman had given up trying to control the rig's swaying progress, and was clutching the support arm of its canopy in sheer terror.

After several attempts to get hold of the reins Harker reckoned that there was only one way of stopping the charging horse and that was to get on board the buggy. There was little time in which to achieve the switch from saddle to seat, because not far ahead the slope dropped steeply and already the edge of the rocky basin into which the buggy would plunge was showing. He had seconds to get on board the buggy to prevent it from plunging into the basin.

Harker leaped from his horse at the same second that the buggy lurched away from him, widening the gap he had to bridge. He feared that the power of his leap was not sufficient to propel him far enough to close the wider distance. He would fall short, and the buggy would plunge off the embankment, inflicting death or terrible injury on the hapless woman.

Harker's fingers grabbed hold of the buggy's canopy. The woman's pale and terrified face flashed in front of him as he swung on to the buggy, just as the canopy disintegrated. The woman's support gone, she swayed backwards, and would have pitched out of the rig were it not for Harker bundling her in a pile under him.

'Lie flat out!' he commanded, and scrambling to his feet, balancing on a knife-edge, he leaped on to the horse and veered the buggy away from its headlong dash off the slope. It took another minute's hair-raising race along the edge of the slope during which at any second the rig could still be pitched to a bloody ending, before he managed to get the horse under control and calmed. He brought the wild-eyed creature to a halt. Aching and spent, he collapsed back on the seat of the rig.

'You damn fool!' the woman rebuked him fierily. 'Galloping helter-skelter on a trail that's only fit for plodding on!'

'And you were acting like you owned the darn road!' Harker flung back. 'Prim and proper and strutting like a queen.'

They stared each other down for a spell before the woman, calmer, said:

'I suppose the most important thing is that we're both alive.'

Bob Harker let go of his anger.

'I guess.'

'That was dare-devil riding just now.'

'Didn't have much choice,' Harker said.

'Another man wouldn't have been as brave.'

Harker grinned. 'Or as dumb, you could say.'

The woman laughed. 'You're a stranger to these parts.' It was a statement, not a question. 'Passing through?'

'If I don't find work.'

'Doing what?'

Harker shrugged. 'Nursing cows. That's what you do in cow country.'

'Would you work in a general store?

Clerking and chores.'

Harker was not enthusiastic.

'Are you one of those men who think that clerking isn't work befitting a man?'

'I don't know anything about clerking. Chores, I've done plenty.'

'My pa owns the general store in town.' Her smile lit her blue eyes and made them dance like sun on water. 'I figure that I could talk him in to getting a younger back to lift those sacks of flour, I do the clerking now, but I won't be around for much longer. So I could teach you to take over.'

'Are you leaving town, ma'am?' Harker enquired, feeling a twinge of disappointment.

She gently scolded.

'Less of the ma'am. I'm only twenty-two.'

'Sorry. Didn't mean to offend you. Wouldn't have if I had a name.'

'Jess, for Jessica, Blossom.'

'Blossom?'

'Blossom,' she restated drily.

'Sure, Jess . . . ' He grinned. 'Blossom, it is.'

'And take that snigger out of your voice!' she commanded.

'You didn't answer my question, Jess.'

'And what question would that be?'

'About leaving town.'

'Leaving town, yes. But not going far. Getting married.'

There was no good reason why he should be so keenly disappointed, but Bob Harker was.

'And you are?' she demanded.

'Harker's the name, Jess. Bob Harker.'

'Where from? My pa will want to know.'

'Wyoming.'

'Good. If you were from Utah, he'd probably shoot you on sight.'

'Why Utah?' Harker asked.

Jess Blossom shrugged. 'Don't know. Pa never said.'

'Didn't you ever ask?'

'No,' she said flatly. 'One thing you'll soon learn about my pa is that he tells you if he wants to. And if he doesn't want to, you'd better not ask. And that's a lesson you should learn quickly, if you go to work for him.'

'Sounds like a pretty determined sort of fella,' was Harker's observation.

'Pa doesn't take offence easily. But given cause, he's as ornery a critter as you're likely to cross paths with. Are you interested in working for him?'

'Never clerked before,' Harker said doubtfully.

'Why don't you drop by the store tomorrow,' Jess suggested. 'Talking costs nothing. But . . . '

'Yes,' Harker prompted, to overcome Jess Blossom's hesitancy.

'When my pa's around you'll have to call me ma'am. He doesn't approve of familiarity by strangers or employees.'

'Seems to me that your pa's kind of . . . '

'Kind of what?'

'Over-protective.'

'I'm all Pa's got.'

Jess Blossom's brow furrowed, and she was suddenly sad.

'Something troubling you, Jess?' Harker enquired, eager to help if he could.

Jess Blossom sighed wearily. 'Three weeks from Sunday. That's my wedding-day.'

'Lucky fella, I'd say,' Bob Harker genuinely complimented.

Jess Blossom blushed. 'First you almost kill me, and now you're sweet-talking me,' she blustered.

'I'm only telling the truth as I see it, Jess,' Harker said sincerely. His glance took in the decrepit buggy. 'This rig is pretty much done for, I'd say. Might I take the liberty of suggesting that you allow me to give you a ride to where you're going. Then I'll come back and try and get the rig back on the road, if it doesn't fall apart in the attempt.'

'I suppose that would be the best solution, Bob,' she said.

'I'll fetch my horse.'

Jess Blossom on board, Harker said: 'If you don't mind my saying so, Jess, for a girl about to get married, you don't seem so keen on the idea.'

'I can't wait, Bob,' she exclaimed. 'But ... well, Pa doesn't exactly approve of my choice of husband.' Jess was amazed at herself, that she should be confiding in a man she had only just met.

'Oh, it isn't anything serious, I'd say.'

'You would?'

'Sure. If I was your pa, I wouldn't want you leaving my house either.'

'You think that that's all it is? Pa is going to miss me that much?'

'Well, I know I would if I was him, Jess.'

'Silly old fool,' Jess Blossom said fondly. 'I'll be by 'most every day.'

Bob Harker grinned. 'You know, Jess, for a man having all of the pie for so long, it's kind of hard for him to get used to smaller portions.'

Jess laughed. 'I swear, Bob Harker, that you must have been born with snake-oil on your tongue.'

It pleased Harker to see the glow of pleasure in Jess Blossom's eyes. And he surely had his regrets that he had not arrived in the territory before another man had put his brand on her.

'Where to, Jess?' he asked in a melancholic tone.

'The Broken Arrow ranch,' she stated, and quickly asked on seeing his reaction: 'Is something the matter, Bob?'

'Reckon not.'

'Do you know how to get to the Broken Arrow?' Jess asked, as they set off.

Harker hunched his shoulder as he took in a heavy breath.

'That I do,' he confirmed. And, running a finger inside his shirt collar, added: 'That I surely do, Jess.'

'There's a short cut,' Jess informed Harker a short time later. 'Through Snake Gorge. Take a left turn just up ahead, near that leaning oak.'

Bob did as he was instructed. Not far on they came to a narrow, twisting passage, bounded on both sides by steep rock-faces that ran unbroken for the length of the passage, showing only short sections of the terrain ahead.

'Snake Gorge?' he enquired of Jess.

'That's what it's called.'

'The name suits the place,' Harker opined.

A short distance into the gorge, Stan Baker suddenly appeared from an off-shoot, closely followed by Bengy Smallwood, each looking as mean as a rattler with its rattle stood on. The hardcases were hiding out in the gorge. Harker tensed, and his hand dropped to his sixgun.

'Oh, it's only Stan and Bengy,' Jess declared, in a friendly and familar manner.

'Friends of yours, Jess?' Harker asked, surprised.

'Well, no. I wouldn't say friends.'

'That's a heck of a relief,' Harker grated.

Before Jess could quiz him further, Baker blocked their progress threateningly and addressed Jess.

'Howdy, Miss Blossom.' His gaze travelled from her to Harker. 'You OK?'

'Yes,' Jess said, puzzled by the cross-currents of animosity passing between the Broken Arrow employees and Bob Harker. 'Why wouldn't I be? What's bothering you fellas?' *Fellas* included Harker.

'I guess me and Stan are surprised by the company you're keepin', Miss Blossom,' Bengy Smallwood said. 'I reckon that Mr Collins wouldn't like it. You figure so, Stan?'

'I'd say that he'd be mighty displeased, Bengy.'

'Will someone tell me what's going on?' Jess demanded, including all three men in her sweeping gaze.

Harker provided the answer.

'These fellas, along with a couple of other Broken Arrow *hombres*, tried to lynch me, Jess.'

Jess Blossom's blue eyes opened saucer-wide.

'They what?'

'We wouldn't call it a lynching,' Smallwood said. 'We'd call it a just hanging.'

'Just hangings come after a judge and jury have their say,' Harker barked.

'Now, just wait a minute.' All eyes switched to Jess. 'Why was Bob being lyn . . . *justly* hanged?'

'That's plumb easy to figure, Miss Blossom,' Baker scoffed. 'He was on Broken Arrow range, despite clear warning that he shouldn't be.'

'You've seen the notices, Miss Blossom?' Smallwood said. 'States clearly that if you trespass, you hang.'

'I've seen the notices Butch posted,' Jess agreed. 'But I figured that they were just to scare off intruders. Not that they meant what they said. 'Butch would never agree to a lynching!'

'Hah!' Harker exclaimed. Jess Blossom leaned over Bob Harker's shoulder to look directly at him. 'Collins was right there, Jess.'

Jess swayed. Harker steadied her.

'There must be some mistake,' she declared, when she'd gathered her wits. 'Butch wouldn't lynch a man for simply stepping on Broken Arrow range.'

'I guess I'd have to disagree with you there, Jess,' Bob Harker said. 'I figure that most of the trees on Broken Arrow range have had ropes slung on them at one time or another.'

Jess stiffened.

'I guess, Mr Harker,' she said stiffly, sliding off his horse, 'that if that's your opinion, I'll not trouble you further.'

She looked to Smallwood and Baker.

'Would one of you gentlemen give me a ride to the ranch?'

Baker got in first, much to Smallwood's displeasure.

'That will surely be my pleasure, Miss Blossom.'

Harker watched Jess ride away, hoping for a backwards glance that would give him some hope of a reconciliation down the line when her hackles settled, but he received none. He wondered how Collins could fool what was obviously an intelligent woman, but it seemed by the thorny offence Jess had taken to his opinion of Collins's character that he had successfully done so.

Not trusting the two hardcases with whom Jess had chosen to travel, Harker dogged their trail until they reached the ranch. Satisfied that she was safe, he then made tracks for the nearby town of Hett's Landing.

3

From the second he was sighted on the edge of town folk took a keen interest in Bob Harker. There was nothing new about a stranger in a Western town earning a keen perusal. Strangers sometimes meant trouble. And trail-dusty as Harker was, folk would tag him as a drifter, a species that had a social standing below a mangy dog.

Drifters were often men who were simply restless with their lot and looking for greener pastures, but the common perception was that they were shiftless, workshy no-goods, on the look-out for an easy unearned dollar and with no qualms about bushwhacking any man or woman to get that dollar. Step inside a store and the cash register was closed. Step inside a saloon, and suddenly the bar went dry. And for the length of his stay a drifter had a constant shadow — the local lawman.

Harker rode along the Main Street, the townsfolk huddled whispering as he rode past. And then it suddenly hit him, it wasn't because he looked like a drifter that he had generated such interest, it was because word had reached town about his near-lynching by Butch Collins.

As he passed the sheriff's office he saw Bart Rattigan at the window, obviously none too pleased by his arrival in town. Rattigan vanished from the window, and seconds later stormed out of the law office.

'Mister,' he hailed Harker. 'Hold up!'

Knowing what kind of a stubborn and ornery cuss Rattigan was, Harker never even thought about not drawing rein.

Rattigan glared at the onlookers.

'Ain't you folk got things to do?' he barked. 'Then go and get them done.'

The sidewalks began to clear. Rattigan turned his attention back to Harker.

'You must really want to die, mister,' he growled. 'I figured that by now you'd be burning trail out of the territory.'

'Thought I might linger for a spell, Sheriff.'

'In a pine box? Because that's what'll happen if you hang around here. The next time Butch Collins decides to see you off, he might just use a bullet. Probably in the back, too.'

Harker grinned. 'You don't think too highly of Mr Collins, do you, Sheriff.'

'I don't think too highly of any man who takes the law in his own hands.' Rattigan's scowl intensified to thunderous. 'And neither do I think highly of a man who's careless or stupid enough to cross range in territory where cows and grass come before any man.'

Rattigan's furious grey eyes bore into Harker's green ones. 'This is troubled country, mister. If cows aren't being rustled, homesteads are being burned down and settlers forced out, if not murdered in cold blood. And if one cattle baron ain't shooting trespassers, another is hanging them. Men are edgy. Boundaries haven't been settled. And some, like Collins, reckon that they'd never have enough cows or grass if they managed to push their boundaries all the way to the Rio Grande.'

'You paint a bleak picture, Sheriff Rattigan,' Harker said. 'A fella might get the impression that he's died and gone to hell.'

Rattigan laughed harshly.

'Well if you haven't, the devil has surely come to visit these parts. Which is pretty much the same thing. Because that gives us hell on earth! So my advice to you is to keep going. I might not be around the next time someone decides to sling a lynch rope.'

'I don't need nursing, Sheriff,' Harker said, understanding, but taking exception to Rattigan's putting legs under him out of town.

Bart Rattigan's shoulders slumped wearily.

'If I had a dime for every man who said that, I'd have been able to retire back East with my brother's family long ago,' he said disconsolately.

'How many men has Collins killed?' Harker enquired casually.

'Your guess is as good as mine,' Rattigan said.

'How come he's not behind bars? Or swinging from a gallows?'

'Because he's clever.'

'It wasn't clever trying to hang me,' Harker observed. 'Lynching is murder plain and simple.'

'That's what the law says, sure enough, mister,' the sheriff conceded. 'But the problem is that most around these parts would figure that if a man is stupid enough to enter on range where the penalty for his transgression is clearly stated and buys trouble, then that's exactly what he deserves.'

'Does the same logic apply to the murder of a homesteader, Sheriff?'

'It does.'

'And you stand by and let this happen?'

Hot anger flushed Bart Rattigan's face.

'I'm one man, mister. A small-town sheriff without even a deputy for back-up. But that doesn't stop me from trying to bring law and order.' His beefy shoulders slumped. 'But most times, try is about the best I can manage.

'I'm the law, bound to act according to that law. That means I need proof. And proof is about as hard to come by as snow in July. And even if I got proof, I'd still need an honest jury.' He scoffed. 'Finding twelve men who can't be bought, or who aren't scared, is about as likely an event as the moon falling to earth, fella.'

'Sounds pretty hopeless and downright dangerous, Sheriff,' Bob Harker opined.

'It's both of those things and a whole lot more, mister.'

'A US marshal seems to be called for, I'd say.'

'Two almost got here. One was shot in the back riding into town. The other took a bundle of dollars and kept heading for Mexico.'

31

'Why haven't *you* headed for Mexico, Sheriff? Or have you not been made that kind of an offer?'

Bart Rattigan glared at Harker.

'Right now I'm trying to figure out why I bothered saving your neck from being stretched, mister,' he growled.

Harker cringed. 'Sorry, Sheriff Rattigan.' His apology was instant and sincere. 'Being an honest man, you'd have every right to blast me out of the saddle for what I just said. But, you see, it's been my experience that a lot of lawmen tote a badge as a means to enrich themselves. And it's a darnwell pleasure to meet one who wears his badge with honour and honesty.'

Bart Rattigan's anger eased.

'What you say about some lawmen is true, fella,' he agreed. 'And I can tell you that it's sometimes real hard not to turn a blind eye or grab a bundle of dollars. But I'm hoping that I can do the job the way it should be done for the next six months to my pension.'

He shoved his hat back on his head, his gaze far off.

'I'll be sure glad to shake the rotten dust of this burg off my boots.'

Bob Harker glanced beyond Rattigan to the swaggering, liquored-up trio who were coming from the saloon.

'The tall gingertop is new trash in town,' the sheriff informed Harker. 'He's been hanging round for the last couple of days, mostly in the saloon.'

The trio went into a conversation conducted in asides and sniggers, then the gingertop stepped off the boardwalk and approached, cutting a weaving path as the liquor in his belly dropped to his legs.

'Broken Arrow?' Harker enquired of the sheriff, nodding in gingertop's direction.

'Not yet, but he will be soon enough,' the sheriff grunted.

'Howdy, Sshurruff,' ginger-hair slurred, staggering inelegantly, much to the amusement of his partners and his own amusement once he righted himself.

'Howdy, Lacey,' Rattigan grated. 'A tad early to be the worse for wear, ain't it.' The sheriff's eyes took in the other men, making it clear that his statement included them as well.

'Ain't no concern of yours how we spend our money, Sshuruff,' Lacey snarled.

'That's right,' Rattigan agreed, and then added stonily; 'Unless spending that money makes trouble for decent folk. And I'd surely be interested to find out where you're getting money for liquor, Lacey.'

'Are you sayin' that we ain't decent folk, and that we're robbers, Rattigan?' growled one of the other men, with a face that would scare a vulture.

'I am, Brennan,' Bart Rattigan stated bluntly.

Harker admired the sheriff's direct speech. It took guts. But he could not help but wonder whether such bluntness was the wisest option when he was dealing with drunks, and drunks who were itching for trouble at that.

Brennan's eyes flashed angrily.

'Now ain't that a' insult, fellas,' he barked. 'And a man's got a right to protect his good name, ain't that so?' His question was addressed to Lacey.

'My folks would expect me to stand up for the fam'ly honour, Sheriff,' the third man of the trio said.

'Your folks are polecats, Donegan!' Rattigan grunted. His eyes swept the others. 'All your folks are polecats. Must be to have had you.'

Bob Harker was as stunned as the threatening trio. However, he quickly cottoned on to Rattigan's strategy. He wanted to stun and enrage the men, because goaded men were careless men, and that might help to even up the odds in the event that they needed evening up. At least, Harker reckoned that that was the theory which had prompted the lawman's brashness. However, it looked like his strategy might backfire, because his daring had acted as a sobering agent on the trio, and in the half-minute since Rattigan had delivered his insult they,

35

especially Lacey, had leaped from rotgut lunacy to sober assessment.

'You take that back right this second, Rattigan,' Lacey growled, with not a sign of a slur in his voice.

'Or?' the sheriff flung back.

Lacey stepped back a couple of paces and settled his stance, his right hand hovering in a claw over his .45.

'Or I'll damn well cut you down where you stand!'

The onlookers whom Rattigan had scattered ten minutes previously were reassembling on the boardwalks. More trash were piling out of the saloon. Lacey's partners had stepped aside, content for him to face Rattigan alone. But Harker figured that should Lacey fail, they would take advantage of Rattigan's concentration on the task in hand, and blast him before he could refocus his attention on them.

The men who had come from the saloon also stepped into the street, bringing the total to a round dozen. Rattigan's strategy, if that's what it had been, had spectacularly backfired. What had been a trio of drunks was now a wolfpack ready to pounce. And that gave Harker a problem that he could well have done without.

He had two choices. Fade away. Or stand with Rattigan. And then he was left with only one choice. Rattigan had stepped in to save him from a lynch rope. He was beholden which meant that he could do no less than throw in his lot with him now.

Damn!

Bob Harker slid from his saddle and stood alongside Bart Rattigan.

'This ain't your fight, mister!' Lacey snarled.

'If you know what's good for ya, you'll just keep right on eatin' trail,' was Brennan's advice.

Rattigan looked at Harker.

'You don't owe me anything, if that's what's prodding you into this,' he stated.

'I'd surely prefer not to be involved, Sheriff,' Harker said. 'But you need my help. Because if you had some kind of strategy to upset this trash, it's surely corkscrewed up your behind.'

'Trash!' Lacey fumed.

'With a capital T,' Bob Harker proclaimed.

'You got a name you want put on your headstone,' Lacey grated.

'I've got a name, but I figure that it's not going on any headstone, fella. Now I think it only fair and proper, before you draw iron, that you should know what you're up against.'

'What the hell is this mouthin' off 'bout?' The angry question was Donegan's.

'If you'll permit me a little demonstration, gents,' Harker said. 'It sure would be wise.'

Bob Harker's sixgun flashed from its holster, and three rapid shots punched a perfect line of holes in the saloon's shingle, even though it was swinging in a stiffish breeze. He slid the sixgun back into its holster, and it was a mighty fast eye that could swear that it had ever left it.

Out of the corner of his eye he saw

Bart Rattigan's reaction, and if his stock had been low with the lawman before, it was now at rock bottom. It was obvious that the sheriff was seeing another fast gun that would be added to the Collins list of hardcases sooner rather than later.

Harker broke the stunned silence.

'You'll never clear leather, Lacey,' he intoned hollowly.

'We was just funnin' round, mister,' a scared Brennan croaked, his voice like the scrape of a nail on tin.

'Yeah,' Donegan pitched in. 'We didn't mean no harm, now did we?' he asked Brennan, whose head was shaking fit to come off.

The trio's support from the saloon was melting away faster than a snowball on a griddle, fighting each other to regain the safety of the saloon in awe of Harker's prairie-lightning draw.

'Run scared if you want,' Lacey rebuked his partners. His dark eyes bored into Harker. 'I ain't runnin' no place.'

'This matter is closed,' Harker told him.

'Not in my book, it ain't!' Lacey bellowed.

'You saw how I can shoot,' Harker reminded Lacey.

'I saw, and I still ain't scared,' Lacey flung back.

The fizzing stand-off was interrupted by the arrival of a wagon driven by a man who was standing, craning his neck.

'Jeb!' he called out.

Lacey swung around.

'It is you,' the driver of the wagon hailed. 'I been looking all over for you, brother.'

'And now that you've found me, keep right on rolling!' Lacey grated.

'Keep rolling!' the new arrival exclaimed. 'I've been searching high and low for you these past coupla months. It was just pure luck that I found my way here.'

'I ain't going back to no sod-busting,' Lacey yelled.

'Pa sent me lookin', Jeb.'

'Well, you go home and tell the old bastard that my days behind a plough are done with, Andy. Now git!'

Andy's eyes took in the gunfight scene.

'No, Jeb,' he wailed. He addressed Harker. 'I don't know what's happened here, mister, but Jeb ain't no gunnie. I'm sure that he's right sorry for any offence he's given, sir. Ain't that so, Jeb?'

'No, it damn well ain't.'

Jeb Lacey's hand dived for his sixgun. His weapon was still in its holster when he dropped to his knees and on to his face. Andy Lacey leaped from the wagon, ran to his brother and cradled him in his arms.

'There was no need to kill him, mister,' he accused Harker. 'No need at all. You were fast enough to do anything you liked, besides killing Jeb.'

'He asked for trouble, and he got it,' Harker said coldly.

'I hope you rot in hell,' was Andy Lacey's curse.

Weeping, he dragged his brother's body to the wagon, refusing anyone's help, and loaded him on board under Harker's glare, who still commanded the street in an open invitation to anyone of a mind to challenge him.

There were no challengers.

'I'll bury him on the prairie where he'd want to be buried,' Andy Lacey told Rattigan, when he offered his help.

A sombre crowd watched the wagon roll out of town, decent folk scornful of Harker, saloon-scum admiring him.

Harker watched the mournful scene, unmoved.

Bart Rattigan was among the scornful.

'Pretty fancy gun-work,' he said. 'The kind not learned in a day — even a year.'

'I gave him fair warning, Sheriff,' Harker said, obviously unwilling to accept Rattigan's criticism. 'And,' he added significantly, 'he drew first.'

'Maybe all that proves, Harker, is that you're a more clever killer than most.'

The lawman grimaced. Rattigan's next statement was one of no compromise. 'I'll expect you out of town in an hour!'

'Ordering fellas to quit the town and territory seems to be a favourite pastime with you, Sheriff,' Bob Harker said, steely-eyed.

Bart Rattigan closed the gap between them in a couple of loping strides.

'You know, mister,' he growled. 'Like I said, I'm already regretting saving your neck from that Broken Arrow noose. I stepped in because some men are worth saving.' He snorted. 'I figure now that you aren't one of those men! You do as I tell you, or I'll come looking for you.'

'I wouldn't do that, Sheriff. You're not fast enough.'

'When I come looking, I'll be toting a shotgun,' Rattigan said stonily.

'My horse is tuckered out. Needs rest.'

Rattigan studied the flagging mare.

'I won't punish the horse for your ways,' he said, and amended: 'First light tomorrow.'

A rider from the men who had come from the saloon to watch Lacey's challenge to Harker galloped past to bring the news of the happening in town to Butch Collins, Harker reckoned. Rattigan confirmed as much.

'Collins is always on the look-out for a fast draw,' he stated. 'It's my guess that he'll make you an offer to join the rest of the trash he employs. But you just keep in mind that my ultimatum stands, mister.'

'I'd remind you again, Sheriff, that I gave fair warning to that man.'

'Fair warning my rear end, mister!' Rattigan bellowed. 'You shot Lacey down when you could have as easily winged him, with your kind of gun skills. Now you might claim that it was a justified killing, and by the strict interpretation of the law it could be deemed to be so. But to me, it was murder. Because you didn't have to kill him.'

He strode into the law office and slammed the door, but not before restating: 'First light, mister!'

The thorny interlude over, the crowd began to disperse. Harker led his horse to the livery. As he passed the general store he saw a man wearing a storekeeper's apron. The name on the store's shingle was Blossom. The balding, slightly stooped man who was observing him with undisguised distaste was none other than Jess Blossom's pa, he reckoned.

Harker figured that he could forget about clerking.

4

'Mr Collins!'

Alerted and alarmed by the incoming rider's strident summons, Butch Collins spun round. His eyes, which had been soft and friendly when looking at Jess Blossom, now became flinty. The last thing he wanted was trouble while Jess was around. He had been careful always to hide his meaner side when in her company, and had issued strict orders to his men not to bring trouble to his doorstep when Jess was around.

So what did the idiot burning up trail think he was doing!

'Mr Collins!' the rider hailed again.

'Larry,' Butch Collins called to a man leaning on the corral gate, where the rancher had taken Jess to select a horse as a gift for her upcoming birthday. Collins's eyes flashed towards the house, indicating that Larry should divert the rider.

'We can do this later, Butch,' Jess said when Larry ran to do as Collins wanted. Her excited blue-eyed gaze took in the many fine horses on offer. 'With all this magnificent horseflesh to choose from, it'll give me more time to think.'

The rancher shrugged.

'No. Larry can deal with whatever it is Riley's got so het up about. That's what I pay him for. Now, look again, Jess.'

'I'd feel better looking, if you attended to business first, Butch,' Jess said, and laughed. 'After all, it won't be long now when what happens at the Broken Arrow will concern me too.'

'You mustn't worry your pretty head about the day-to-day affairs of the ranch, Jess. All you'll have to do is look pretty and bear me fine sons.'

Being a woman of independent thought and view, Butch Collins's perception of her role as his wife did not settle easy with Jess Blossom.

'I don't want to be just an ornament, Butch,' she warned, her face set in determined lines. 'I want to play a full part in the running of the Broken Arrow.'

'And you will,' Collins soothed.

'Don't humour me, Butch. I mean what I say. And if you don't agree, now is the time to say so.'

He drew her into his arms.

'Of course I agree, Jess,' he crooned. 'I wouldn't want it any other way, other than having you at my side, us running the Broken Arrow together.'

Relieved and pleased, Jess Blossom snuggled up to her soon-to-be husband.

'That sure pleases me greatly, Butch,' she sighed.

Had she been able to look into her future husband's eyes then she would have run away faster than Riley had ridden in, because she would have seen in their mean depths the inner mean-tempered and cruel man which he had, in the year they had been courting, carefully hidden. Butch Collins needed a wife to bear him the sons he needed to secure the long-term future and expansion of the Broken Arrow when, as he planned, to run for high political office. And he also needed a woman who would be perfect in the role of, he hoped, a Washington wife one day. Jess Blossom had points to spare in all departments.

When he had formulated his plans for the Broken Arrow and his future as a politician, he had looked around, the way he might for good stock. And had considered himself very fortunate when he saw Jess Blossom.

There was only one problem that just might disrupt his plans, and that problem was old man Blossom.

'Has your pa got any kinder to having me as his son-in-law, Jess?' he now asked, with a quiet tenseness.

'Oh, he'll come round, Butch. Never you worry.'

Collins held his bride-to-be at arm's length.

'And what if he doesn't, Jess?'

Jess looked away from his stare.

'He will, Butch,' she said, more in hope than certainty.

The rancher turned her face to his.

'Will you go against your pa, if he doesn't, Jess?' And when Jess shifted uneasily, he pressed: 'I need to know, Jess. I don't want to end up looking the fool of all fools. A man's got his pride to consider.'

'I'll talk to him again, the minute I get back to town, Butch.'

'That's not an answer to the question I asked, Jess,' he said sharply.

'I'm of full age, and he can't stop me marrying you, Butch,' Jess stated.

'That's still not an answer!'

'I'll marry you, Butch,' Jess Blossom promised, after a moment's intense reflection. 'Even if my pa's against our union.'

He chuckled. 'That's my girl. I just knew the first time I set eyes on you that you had the kind of spit in you that I need in my woman, Jess.'

He kissed her passionately. But strangely, Jess felt none of the fire that had been there previously when he kissed her. She would hate having to disobey her pa, but that was not the only concern she had. What really puzzled and troubled her was the way Bob Harker crept into her thoughts. And not for the first time since they had so dramatically met.

★　★　★

The subject of Jess Blossom's thoughts was at that moment of a like mind as far as she was concerned, as he made his way to the town livery, not liking one little bit Art Blossom's despising glare as he went past the general store. He tipped his hat in a friendly manner, but Blossom ignored the gesture of cordiality. He swung around, entered the store and slammed the door, making it clear that neither Harker's patronage or person was welcome. All in all, he was now out of favour with both Blossoms.

The livery-keeper was a tad more welcoming, as business, going by the empty stalls, was not booming. But Bob Harker reckoned that if business had even been marginally better, his welcome in these quarters would be every bit as stinting as it was at the general store.

'How long will ya be stayin' round?' the livery-keeper asked, his eyes going all the way along the street in the direction of the sheriff's office. Obviously Bart Rattigan was impatient with troublemakers, and the livery man was already guessing that he had given Harker his marching orders.

'A spell,' Harker said.

'How long is a spell, mister?'

'Depends,' Harker said, not giving anything away.

'On what?' the keeper pressed sourly, annoyed by Harker's parsimony with information.

Harker's hackles were raised a touch

too by the livery-keeper's harping.

'On when I feel like quitting this excuse for a town. Is that plain enough for you?'

'No need to bite my head off,' the keeper groused.

'Well, it ain't polite to press a man for information he doesn't want to give.'

'Pick your stall.' The keeper stepped aside. 'Feed?'

'The best oats.'

'That'll cost ya. Plenty,' the keeper emphasized.

Harker snorted. 'Never figured otherwise.'

With his horse safely housed, Harker took a stroll along the main street to the saloon. As saloons went, the Dancing Lady was grubbier than most and its whiskey was lousier than any he'd tasted before. It burned all the way down and then exploded in the belly, sending waves of sour heat up Harker's throat. His mouth tasted of ashes.

'What's the main ingredient of this?' Harker quizzed the barkeep, holding the glass up to the light that was struggling to penetrate the greasy and dust-clogged window. 'Mule's piss!'

'Don't have to drink it if you don't want,' the barkeep grunted, rubbing the top of his completely bald head with a grimy bar-cloth.

'You be careful now,' Harker chuckled. 'There's enough dirt on that cloth to grow your hair.'

The barkeep grabbed the bottle on the bar from which he had poured Harker's drink and moved away to the far end, his eyes never leaving Harker for a second. The barkeep was not making a point, Harker figured, because since he had entered the saloon imbibers had been slowly drifting away, until now there was enough empty space around him to hold a barn dance in.

Harker casually leaned on the bar, giving no hint of any concern on his part. From under the brim of his hat he glanced in the mirror behind the bar coated with fly-shit, and saw a man detach himself from a group in the saloon's shadiest corner. He came forward to stand behind Harker, who seemingly remained unperturbed by the man's threatening stance.

'Can I do something for you, fella?' Harker enquired lazily.

The man's tongue ran over lips made dry by the apprehension churning his gut.

'You're pretty fast with that gun,' he said, a crack in his voice that made it sing-song.

Harker snorted. 'I'm a whole lot better than *pretty* fast.' He swung around from the bar. 'I'm greased-lightning fast.' He settled steely eyes on the man. 'So I'd say that you should consider that fact before you draw, if that's what you've got in mind.'

The patrons of the Dancing Lady melted into the saloon's corners.

'I'm kinda fast m'self, friend.'

'I'm not your friend,' Harker intoned.

'I figure that I might even be faster,' the man said.

'You'll be in hell before you'll find

out that you're not,' Harker said, in the easy and unworried manner of a man who has total confidence in his ability.

Beads of sweat broke on his challenger's forehead.

'Let it be, mister,' Harker said. 'You're not near fast enough.'

The man was at a crossroads, dithering between his eagerness to make a reputation, and his fear of dying. And there was a third element, the one which would probably drive him to draw irrespective of his chances of success, and that was his pride — a devil on his back. He could be one of two things. The toast of the town. Or, if he backed down, the town fool.

Harker tensed, figuring that pride would probably win out.

⋆　⋆　⋆

Butch Collins kept his goodfellow grin fixed in place while he waved off Jess Blossom on the mare she had selected from the corral. But when Jess was far enough away he swung around and went thunderously to the house, marching straight to the den where Riley and Larry were awaiting his presence.

'Did you bring news of the end of the world, Riley!' he bellowed. He rammed a fist in the unfortunate ranny's face and sent him sprawling to the floor on the far side of the spacious den. 'Disturing the peace like you did when Miss Blossom was visiting.'

Riley staggered to his feet, not sure if the moon had dropped on his head.

'S-s-sorry, Mr Collins,' he stammered. 'But I figgered you'd want to know 'bout what I seen in town.'

The rancher's anger lost some of its fire to curiosity.

'What happened in town?'

'I just seen the fastest draw I ever seen, Mr Collins,' the excited Riley said.

The last of Butch Collins's anger lost out to his interest in Riley's story.

'How fast?'

'So fast that I hardly seen it,' Riley said.

'Interesting,' was the rancher's response.

Riley, his fear of Collins's wrath easing, said, 'I figgered you'd want to hire this gent, Mr Collins. That's why I burned trail here, 'cause Bart Rattigan's given him 'til first light to hit the trail. If he waits that long, 'cause he's in one bitch of a mood, is the sheriff.'

'You did right, Riley,' Collins said. 'Give the man a drink,' he ordered Larry. And saddle my horse.' He questioned Riley closely. 'Faster than the eye can see, you say?'

'Like I said, Mr Collins, I ain't never seen no one faster. Gunned that bar-bum Lacey 'fore he could blink.'

Butch Collins's eagerness dropped a notch.

'Lacey, huh? A man wouldn't have to be that fast to outdraw a drunk.'

'Ya gotta see what I seen, Mr Collins,' Riley said, gulping down the generous whiskey that Larry had poured.

'Well, I'd better go and see then, hadn't I,' Collins murmured, preoccupied with his thoughts.

If the man was as fast as Riley claimed

he was, he could be the bogeyman he'd been looking for to put legs under neighbours who had remained unpersuaded up to now. Baker and Smallwood were hardcases, true enough, but they were not out of the top drawer of desperadoes. Those special kinds of trouble-stirrers had fast-thinking brains as well as quick-shooting guns.

Riding away from the ranch, Butch Collins was hoping that the fast gun in town had all the qualities that would make him the kind of ace enforcer he'd been searching for; the kind of mean-tempered, quick-thinking, fast-gun *hombre* that would help him to extend the boundaries of the Broken Arrow to the point where its borders could no longer be reached unless a man had time counted in days instead of hours.

★   ★   ★

The tension in the Dancing Lady crackled. A breathless stillness pervaded the saloon.

'You've got the same choice as Lacey had,' Bob Harker told his challenger. 'You can just walk away.'

'I ain't no quitter,' the man said, a shake in his voice that made it reedy.

'There's no future in being dead,' Harker said.

Knowing that he had overstepped the mark, the man's eyes were now haunted by fear. And the beads of sweat on his forehead had become a glossy sheen all over his face.

'You can take that bastard, Jimmy,' a voice called from a far corner.

Bob Harker doubted that the man's urging sprang from confidence in Jimmy's gun skills. Rather, he reckoned that the man, excited by the prospect of a gunfight, did not want that excitement snatched away should the confrontation fizzle out.

Harker saw the tell-tale change in the man's eyes that told him he had gone beyond reason and, now driven by an urge close to insanity, he had become convinced that he had the measure of

Harker. Another second and guns would have blasted, were it not for the appearance of Bart Rattigan's shotgun-toting figure in the batwings.

'Two barrels, two bodies,' the Hett's Landing sheriff growled.

5

The tension in the saloon reached a pitch, and might have exploded into violence had not Butch Collins joined Bart Rattigan.

'Back off, Jimmy,' Collins said, addressing Bob Harker's challenger.

The man called Jimmy put on a brief show of reluctance, but he fooled no one. His relief at having been extricated from a situation that foolishness and pride had goaded him in to was there in the relaxation of his every nerve and muscle.

'Sure, Mr Collins,' he said. 'If that's what you want.'

Normally it would be the last thing Butch Collins would want. But he had come to town to investigate Riley's story, and was stunned when, turning Harker's way, he saw who was reputed to be this fast draw Riley spoke of.

'You!' Butch Collins exclaimed. 'You're this fast draw that my man Riley spoke of?'

'Faster than prairie lightning, Mr Collins,' a snivelling bar-bum said, licking lips that had not tasted whiskey for over an hour. 'I seen him draw, sir.'

Collins distanced himself from the bar-bum, his nostrils flaring at the man's stench.

'Harry,' he called to the barkeep, 'give him a drink.'

The bar-bum's tortured eyes lit up. He sidled up to the bar, a man whose pride had long ago been crushed by his addiction.

'I figure that this matter is concluded, Sheriff,' Collins told Bart Rattigan.

Rattigan's hackles were at full stretch, but he had the wisdom not to reignite trouble by standing on ceremony. He backed out of the saloon, his glare fixed on Harker, letting there be no doubt that he saw Harker as a thorn that would have to be plucked, and plucked soon.

'I'll see you in my office in ten minutes, Harker,' the sheriff commanded, and added significantly: 'And I'll expect your horse to be hitched to the rail outside, ready for the trail.'

'We agreed on first light tomorrow, Sheriff,' Harker said.

'This town has had too many funerals of late,' Rattigan flung back. 'Without you adding to the total, mister!'

Butch Collins glanced over the top of the batwings after Rattigan, grinning.

'I do declare that that Bart Rattigan can be a mighty thorny customer.'

'I guess he's just trying to uphold the law,' Bob Harker said. The rancher swung around.

'That sounds to me like you're backing the sheriff, fella?' His gaze on Harker was probing.

Harker shrugged. 'I've got a lot to thank the sheriff for,' he said. 'After all, if he hadn't happened along when he did, my neck would be a whole lot longer than it is now.'

Collins stiffened, but reckoning that there were more flies caught by honey than by vinegar, he let go of his anger.

'That would have been a bad mistake by me, I reckon,' he chuckled. 'Because then I wouldn't be able to hire you.'

Now it was Bob Harker's turn to laugh.

'Hire me?' he questioned, as if struck by a bolt of lightning. 'Now why would you want to do that, Collins?'

'Simple. You're a fast gun. And I need a fast gun,' said the rancher with direct bluntness.

'That I've seen, you've already got all the gun talent you need in Stan Baker and Bengy Smallwood.'

The rancher sighed. 'Sure, having Baker and Smallwood on the Broken Arrow payroll has had its benefits. But they're hardcases. And there's a world of difference between an everyday hardcase and a skilled gunfighter.'

'I'm not a gunfighter,' Harker corrected.

'Maybe not by profession, in the

strict sense of the word,' Collins said. 'But you didn't get that fast draw I've heard about by wearing a gun for fashion.'

The bar-bum was back.

'Put three holes in a straight line in the saloon shingle, while it was swayin' in the breeze, Mr Collins,' he said.

This time Collins was not of a generous frame of mind and shoved the bar-bum aside, sending the wobbly-legged drunk sprawling. His head collided with the brass footrail of the bar, and he lay on the ground moaning.

'Throw him out!' the rancher bellowed.

Bob Harker stepped in front of the three willing and eager men who hurried forward to do Butch Collins's bidding. The men stopped and cast a glance back to Collins. The rancher nodded them away. Harker picked up the drunk and steadied him.

'Whiskey, barkeep,' he ordered.

The barkeep filled a one-shot glass and, drawing deeply from his nasal passages, contemptuously spat across the bar. The barkeep's snot landed on the leg of the drunk's trousers.

'Leave it, friend,' Harker commanded, when the drunk went to wipe the mucus off. He slid the half-filled bottle of rotgut the drunk's way.

The man's eyes filled with tears.

'I thank you for your kindness, stranger,' he said, hugging the bottle to his chest.

'It's no kindness I do you,' Harker said. 'There's a devil in that bottle that you should spill out right now.'

The drunk shook his head sadly.

'The devil owns me, mister.' He slouched away to a dark corner of the saloon.

'Hold up!' Harker turned to the barkeep. 'I reckon you should take back what you gave that gentleman just now, barkeep.'

The barkeep was genuinely puzzled.

'And I also reckon that you should put it right back where you got it from, too.'

The barkeep's puzzlement deepened.

'Don't know what you're talking about,' he railed.

'Then let me show you.' Harker reached across the bar, grabbed the barkeep by the apron and dragged him over the bar and hauled him to where the drunk was waiting. Harker pointed to the green slime on the drunk's trouser leg. 'Lick it off!'

'It ain't no problem, mister,' the drunk said, obviously fearing a terrible retribution when Harker was not around. He reached down to wipe away the snot.

'Leave it,' Harker said, and told the barkeep, 'I don't want to have to make you lick it off, fella.'

'Now wait a minute!'

Bob Harker glared at Butch Collins. 'You want me to work for you, right?'

'Sure.'

Harker delivered an ultimatum: 'Then the barkeep does as I say. And from here on in, shows respect to this gentleman.'

Though Harker's ultimatum clearly went against the grain, Collins instructed the barkeep: 'Do as the man says, Harry.'

'But, Mr Col — '

Foul-tempered, Butch Collins grabbed the barkeep and forced him on to his knees.

'Like the man says, Harry. Lick it off!'

Task completed, the barkeep rushed outside to vomit.

'Satisfied?' Collins enquired of Harker. 'What do they call you?'

'Harker. Bob Harker.'

'Well, Harker, I've got a ranch to run. Let's hit the trail back to the Broken Arrow.'

'Aren't you getting ahead of yourself, Mr Collins?' Harker said.

'Don't see how,' the rancher barked impatiently.

'I haven't agreed to work for you yet.'

Butch Collins was genuinely taken aback. It obviously had not occurred to him that any man would turn down the chance to work for the Broken Arrow.

'You saying you won't?' was his challenge.

Bob Harker grinned. 'A long way, isn't it,' he mused, 'from wanting to string me up a couple of hours ago, to wanting to hire me now.'

'Times change, circumstances change,' Collins said pragmatically. 'That's the way of things round these parts.' He held Harker's gaze. 'So, what's it to be? Work for me, or risk me hanging you?'

Harker turned to the bar, turning his back on Butch Collins, who did not like the idea one little bit.

'No rush. I'll think about,' he said, as if the rancher's offer was a long way down the line in his list of priorities.

'When you make up your mind,' Collins growled, 'I might not be of a mind to hire you, Harker!'

'That's a chance I'll have to take, I guess,' Harker drawled. He swung around from the bar. 'But I reckon that any time I'm willing to sign on, you'll be hiring the kind of talent I've got.'

The saloon crowd were aghast at Harker's effrontary. Not many men had dressed down Butch Collins. And the few who had been brave enough or stupid enough to try were no longer above ground. Everyone awaited the rancher's reaction with bated breath, most figuring that it would be swift and harsh. Their surprise was total when, with a grunt, Collins said benignly:

'You figure, huh?'

'I do,' Bob Harker replied confidently.

'Now why do you think that I'd kowtow to you, Harker?'

'Simple. You need my gun to enforce your plans.'

Stumped and conscious of eyes on him, Butch Collins turned and strode angrily out of the Dancing Lady saloon.

'Doggone,' an old-timer supping at the bar said, awed. 'Never knowed Butch Collins to take lip like that, mister,' he told Harker.

'Seen him kill or horsewhip men for a

whole lot less,' another equally stunned man said.

'You'd better watch moving shadows from now on, Mr Harker,' a rotund man garbed in a frock-coat warned. He proferred his hand. 'Doc Julius Speare.'

Harker took his hand to shake.

'Nice meeting you, Doc.'

Speare's attitude of bonhomie changed. 'Are you going to ride for the Broken Arrow, Mr Harker?'

'Like I said, I haven't made up my mind.'

'If you do, don't expect me to patch up any holes in you. Because I figure that any man who ties up with Butch Collins deserves what ever fate befalls him.'

'That states it clearly, Doc,' Harker drawled.

'I like a man to know where he stands.' The doc grabbed a bottle of whiskey off the bar. 'Now, while you're making up your mind, why not share this bottle with me, Mr Harker.'

He poured a generous drink.

'If you're so opposed to Collins, how come you're still sucking air, Doc?' was Bob Harker's genuinely curious question.

'I suspect he wants to keep me around, just in case he catches lead himself.'

'I thought you said that you'd not treat any Broken Arrow man?'

'I did.'

'So your high-principled stand applies only to Broken Arrow hirelings, and not the bossman himself?'

'That's so.'

'Seems kind of unfair to me,' Harker opined.

'Well,' Doc Speare slugged liberally of his whiskey with the relish of a man who had a fondness for liquor, evidenced by the prominent veins on his face, 'the way I see it is that Butch Collins was born the way he is and can't do much about it. Other men, men like you, Harker, have a choice. You exercise your free will. And in my book, if you need doctoring, then you damn well better be able to heal yourself. Do I make myself clear, Mr Harker?'

'Perfectly,' Harker said.

'Another drink?'

Bob Harker shook his head. 'I've just decided to hire out to Collins, Doc.'

Doctor Julius Speare pulled the half-empty bottle to him. 'Thank you for your honesty, sir,' he said.

* * *

Jess Blossom hurried from the general store to intercept Butch Collins as he strode from the saloon.

'Butch, why didn't you ride to town with me? If you were coming so soon.'

'My plans changed,' he said grumpily, the way he sometimes did, and that worried Jess. At such times he seemed downright dismissive of her views and her presence.

'Did Seth Riley change them?' she quizzed closely.

'What if he did?'

Jess flinched.

'You've got to understand, Jess. Ranching isn't like running a general store. Sometimes decisions have to be taken quickly. A man's got to strike while the iron is hot, you might say. And sometimes those decisions aren't liked very much. But that's the way it is in cow country.'

He vaulted into the saddle.

'You'll get to understand that when you're my wife.'

Jess Blossom lost some of the glow that the prospect of being Mrs Butch Collins used to bring her. The rancher, curious as to what she was looking at behind him, turned in his saddle to see Bob Harker coming from the saloon.

'I'm ready to ride for the Broken Arrow, Mr Collins,' he said.

'I never doubted that you would, Harker,' Butch Collins said smugly.

'Ride for the Broken Arrow?' Jess said, stunned.

'Sure thing, Jess — '

'That'll be Miss Blossom to you,

Harker,' Collins snarled, his stare furious.

'Mr Collins has offered me a job,' he finished for Jess's benefit.

'I offered you a job,' Jess said, miffed.

'No, you didn't, *Mizz* Blossom,' he corrected. 'You figured that your pa might.' He looked across the street to the grim-faced storekeeper and grinned. 'And I reckon that he's not of a mind to. Besides,' he strolled to his horse, 'clerking isn't my bailiwick, ma'am.'

'I guess it's not at that, Mr Harker,' Jess Blossom said frostily, her gaze fixed pointedly on Harker's Colt sixgun.

'I'll drop by the house this coming Sunday, Jess,' Collins promised.

Jess shrugged. 'If you're of a mind to, Butch.'

Collins studied her. 'Of course I'm of a mind to, Jess. Soon you'll be Mrs Butch Collins.' Jess glanced anxiously behind her to her pa. 'The old man's still not of a welcoming mood, huh?'

'Pa will come round, Butch.'

'There isn't much time left to do

that, Jess. And I sure hope that if he remains opposed to the idea of having me as a son-in-law, that you'll have the sense to pitch him to blazes.'

He swung his horse. 'Let's ride, Harker!'

Bob Harker tipped his hat. 'Be seeing you around, Miss Blossom.'

Heavy-hearted, Jess watched the two men ride out, regretting, though she wasn't sure why, that Bob Harker had thrown in his lot with the Broken Arrow. And she worried that her feelings for Butch Collins did not seem to be as vibrant as they had been, even a short time ago.

'What in tarnation's got into you, Jess Blossom,' she said angrily, and flounced off to the general store.

'Well-matched, I'd say,' Art Blossom said, casting his eyes after Harker and Collins.

Jess had nothing to say. She brushed past her pa and took up her bookkeeping where she had left off, her mind as scattered as leaves in a fall gale.

Observing her flustered mood, her pa asked:

'Are you still intent on marrying that fella Collins, Jess?'

'Of course I am, Pa,' she said impatiently.

'You don't reckon that it would be a big mistake?'

'No! I love Butch.'

'And you'll marry him against my wishes, Jess?'

'Butch is a fine man, Pa,' Jess claimed. 'And I'm a very fortunate woman that he's chosen me to be his wife. You should be happy and glad for me, instead of all the time doing Butch down.' She shook her head vehemently, spilling her blond hair across her shoulders. 'I honestly don't know what bee you've got in your bonnet about Butch, Pa. I really don't!'

'Life, having put a lot of grey in my hair, has also put wisdom in my head, Jess,' Art Blossom said, in the quiet way he did when underlining the point he wanted to make. 'And a man comes to recognize another man who claims to be what he's not.'

'You're talking in riddles, Pa,' Jess wailed.

'It's only a riddle if you don't want to listen to me or, I suspect, your heart, Jess.'

'Butch Collins is a good man, Pa,' Jess Blossom restated fiercly. 'And I'm going to marry him!'

'Even if you're hankering after another man?' her pa accused.

'Hankering after another man! And who might that be?'

'That fella with the lightning-fast gun,' Blossom stated.

'Eyewash, Pa! And now you're making me skyhigh mad.'

Jess put down her pen, seeing no point at all in further messing up the accounts ledger, the book was already bearing the evidence of her wandering mind since she had arrived back in town and had heard of the events during her absence, frankly surprised and deeply perturbed by Bob Harker's part in those events.

Art Blossom was shaking his head in open wonder.

'Never knew a woman who picked so many lame ducks.'

'I was in love with Billy Clanton,' Jess said defensively, at mention of the man in her life before Butch Collins.

'He might have been in love with you, too,' the storekeeper said, 'if he was sober long enough to realize it.'

'So if you compare Butch to Billy, one a drunk and the other a big rancher, I reckon you should be over the moon that I saw sense, Pa.'

Art Blossom sighed, heavy-shouldered. 'Well, at least Billy Clanton was at heart a good man.'

'Meaning that Butch isn't?' Jess challenged.

'Meaning that Butch Collins has a veneer that covers rot inside,' he stated bluntly. 'And badness inside eventually seeps through to the outside, Jess.'

'I'm not going to listen to any more of this, Pa,' Jess said sternly, and flashed past him on her way out of the store.

'I saw the way you looked at that gun-slick fella just now, Jess.'

Jess spun around at the door.

'OK. What if I married Bob Harker instead of Butch Collins?'

'Frying pan to the fire,' Blossom replied.

'You know what I think,' Jess said hotly. 'I think that you don't want me to marry any man at all. You want me right here with you, cooking and washing and sewing. And doing the books and the chores.'

Art Blossom flinched under his daughter's stinging tirade.

'The look you saw on my face outside was surprise and, yes, disappointment too, that Bob Harker had hired on as a gun to the Broken Arrow. Because I figured that he was a man of finer qualities. I even told him that I'd ask you if he could have the vacant clerking job.'

'If he's as fast with a nib and ink as he is with a gun, we'd have the best-kept books in the West,' her father opined sarcastically. 'Probably in the whole darn country.' Blossom's eyes narrowed. 'And how come you know so much about this . . . Bob Harker, did you say?'

'It's a long story,' Jess said. 'And right now I'm not of a mind to tell it.'

Jess swept out the door, ignoring her pa's request to explain how she knew so much about Harker. She went quickly to the livery, saddled the fine mare of which Butch Collins had made her a gift, and rode out of town, headed for the creek where she often went to think and ponder in the months before her ma had finally been beaten by the cancer in her stomach.

Seated on a rocker outside the sheriff's office, Bart Rattigan watched with interest Jess Blossom's fiery departure from the general store and her spirited exit from the town. He saw Art Blossom come to the door of the general store to look after his daughter, and even though there was a good distance between the sheriff's office and the general store, there was no mistaking the storekeeper's worried demeanour. Everyone in Hett's Landing was aware of Blossom's opposition to his daughter's marriage to Butch Collins, and, like him, were hoping that Jess would see sense and cancel the wedding. But Rattigan reckoned that, having been disappointed in Billy Clanton, Jess was determined not to have another matrimonial fiasco. One mistake, fellas would forgive. But two, and they might think that the woman was not wife material. Which, were that to happen, would leave Jess Blossom gathering dust on the old maid's shelf.

Western men liked their wives to be exclusive to them, no matter how they tom-catted about. And the suspicion would be, were Jess to falter at her second matrimonial fence, that the man involved had done the decent thing and kept his mouth shut when he had found out that the woman he intended to marry was not as lilywhite as he'd have wished. And all it took for a woman to be consigned to the wilderness of spinsterhood, was even the slightest whiff of suspicion.

From one of his late-night jawing sessions with Art Blossom, Bart Rattigan knew that he worried too about his daughter being left unmarried. In Western society, an unwed daughter was socially undesirable.

'But I'd damn well prefer Jess to be an old maid than see her hitched to Butch Collins,' Blossom had fumed.

As Rattigan looked into the swirling dust left in Jess Blossom's wake, like Art Blossom he wondered about the way Jess had looked at Bob Harker when it became clear that he had decided to ride for the Broken Arrow. It was, to him, the look of a woman struggling with a dilemma of the heart.

Maybe, after all, Jess Blossom would not marry Butch Collins. But would there be any difference if she married Bob Harker?

'Polecat for polecat,' Rattigan murmured, and resumed chewing on the cigar he was smoking.

6

During the ride to the Broken Arrow Butch Collins had not uttered a single word, and that suited Bob Harker, because he had a whole lot of thinking to do. He had successfully infiltrated the Collins outfit.

'There's a whole mess of trouble around Sweetwater Valley,' the territorial governor had said, when he had summoned him two weeks previously. 'Hangings and shootings, and folk with a right to free government land being driven off or buried where they were killed.

'Seems like a rancher by the name of Butch Collins intends to claim the entire valley by fair means or foul. So I reckon that he has to be stopped in his tracks, and that you're the man to do the job.'

'I appreciate your confidence in me,

Governor,' Harker had stated. However, being conscious of the US marshals who had failed to bring order to the murderous environs of Sweetwater Valley, he added: 'But I'd only be interested in taking on the job, if I have free rein in getting the job done.'

For a moment the governor reacted badly to Harker's ultimatum.

'You're a governor's agent,' he reminded Harker. 'And that makes me the boss.'

Harker was not fazed by the governor's digging in his heels.

'It doesn't make any sense to ask a man to root out the rot in a hotbed of murder and mayhem such as Sweetwater Valley, and then tie his hands behind his back by his having to check in with you all the time, Governor,' he stated bluntly. 'With respect,' he continued boldly, 'sitting in the territorial capital, giving orders to a man in the field who might need to make split-second decisions, does not seem to me, at any rate, practical or even remotely sensible. Sir,' he tagged on respectfully.

The governor, not used to having his orders questioned, was taken aback. However, being a pragmatic man who had loftier political ambitions, he knew that the kind of range war that was being waged in Sweetwater Valley would be a black mark on his record that might very well hinder or stop dead in its tracks his climb of the slippery pole of politics. Besides, he knew the man standing before him to be the most efficient and dedicated agent he had. So giving him free rein was not as much of a risk as it would be, were he to afford others the same leeway.

'What have you in mind?' he enquired.

'First off, agents Jeb Lacey and Ned Benton. After that, some slick acting, I reckon.'

The governor's fleshy face took on a frown of concern.

'Slick acting, did you say?'

'Yes, that's what I said, Governor.'

The governor, wise in the ways of

politics, asked no further questions, but placed the full weight of responsibility for the failure of his agent's plans on him. But, as Harker knew, were his scheme to get the required results and Sweetwater Valley was tamed, he'd get none of the credit. The governor was not a man who shared success with anyone.

'Good luck,' the governor said. 'Do me proud.'

'I'll certainly try, Governor,' Harker promised.

Arriving in the region of Sweetwater Valley with Jeb Lacey and Ned Benton, Harker had hidden out in the hills for a couple of days to reconnoitre the valley. And by night he slipped into town to gauge the mood of the town, relative to Butch Collins, whom he had quickly identified as the main protagonist in the troubled valley. A man of gargantuan ambition, he seemed willing to serve the devil's every need and trade his immortal soul for possession of the valley and far beyond. He found in the main, that folk were resigned to the inevitability of Butch Collins ruling the valley and the town, too.

To prevent him, Collins's neighbours would have eventually to adopt his tactics, or up and leave. As yet that decision had not been made, but it was only a matter of time before it was. Then Sweetwater Valley would be Butch Collins's by default. Or a full range war would break out.

As a result of his detective work, it quickly became clear to Bob Harker that to restore order and neighbourly living to town and valley, the viperish Butch Collins would have to be dealt with. So he set about explaining to his fellow agents the role they would play in what he hoped would end in the taming of Butch Collins.

'Jeb, I want you to practise at playing dead,' he told Lacey.

'Dead!' Lacey had yelped, and wanted to know: 'How the hell will that help us to hogtie Butch Collins?'

'You'll see,' Harker promised. And

turning to Ned Benton, he said: 'And I want you to practise at being Jeb's bereaved brother, Ned.'

Like Jeb Lacey, Ned Benton thought that Harker had taken leave of his senses. That was until he filled in the full scenario which he hoped would bring him to Butch Collins's attention, and get him inside the Broken Arrow and right to its rotten core.

'Let me get this straight,' Lacey checked, when Harker had filled in the details of his plan. 'I'll get shot by you in a gunfight in town, and Ned will show up pretending to be my brother who's spent months looking for me?'

Harker nodded.

'Then what?' Ned Benton wanted to know.

'Then I'm hoping that I'll come to Butch Collins's attention. I hear that he's always on the look-out for gun talent to do his dirty work. With you dead, Jeb,' he explained, 'and Ned having supposedly buried you, it'll sure come as a surprise when you make a reappearance.'

Jeb Lacey laughed heartily. 'I'm looking forward to seeing Collins's face.'

'He'll probably drop dead,' Ned Benton said, joining in the other's laughter.

'If he does, it'll save the expense of a hanging, I reckon,' Bob Harker observed.

★ ★ ★

The next day, while monitoring the range for signs of mischief, Harker had seen Bart Rattigan riding across Broken Arrow range, and in a flash came up with a plan to introduce himself to the locale and its key players. He'd have preferred to have the backup of Lacey and Benton to call on should his plan go badly awry, but Jeb Lacey had taken up hanging about the saloon in Hett's Landing, acting the hardcase to set the scene for the fake gunfight with Harker. And Ned Benton was keeping out of sight, drifting between a ridge overlooking Hett's Landing to monitor the happenings there, and watching Harker's back.

Aware of the signs warning that trespassers would be hanged, Harker made a decision to draw Collins into the web he was weaving, gambling on Rattigan's timely intervention to save his neck from being stretched.

He had ridden across the range at the leisurely pace of a man reconnoitering country he might settle in. Not long into his journey, a band of riders charged towards him at a full gallop. The Broken Arrow crew, he figured. He had continued to view the terrain, appearing to pay no heed to the riders until their dust was swirling around him.

Two men leapt from their horses, dragged Harker to the ground and bound his hands behind his back.

Butch Collins came to tower over him snarling, 'You've just earned yourself a rope, mister.'

They hauled him off to a nearby tree.

Harker recalled how he had sweated in those seconds before Rattigan put in an appearance, praying that he had not lost the battle to snare Collins at the first move. And hoping that the sheriff had not drifted off in another direction to the one he had anticipated he'd travel.

When Bart Rattigan showed up the noose was already biting his neck and Harker was the most relieved man in the territory to see the iron-willed sheriff.

He hated deceiving the honest lawman by keeping from him the fact that he was one of the governor's special agents, formed to counter the growing lawlessness that was gripping the territory, a blight that was overwhelming sheriffs and marshals, including US marshals, and making the everyday life of law-abiding citizens a misery, never knowing when they might fall victim to an outbreak of violence, or suffer the loss of their hard-earned possessions.

Besides Bart Rattigan, there was one other person whom Bob Harker wished that he could reveal his true nature and purpose to, and that was Jess Blossom. Her look of disappointment when she had seen him throw in his lot with Butch Collins was both crushing and uplifting; crushing in that he had obviously sunk to an all-time low in her estimation, and uplifting because she cared enough about him to be concerned.

But if she was concerned about him, where did she stand with Butch Collins? The man she was virtually on the eve of marrying. Frankly, what he did or did not do should not worry Jess one iota. Could it be that she was having second thoughts about being Mrs Butch Collins? And if she was, could it remotely mean that he might be the reason for her uncertainty? He realized how big-headed that was, seeing that she hardly knew him.

★ ★ ★

Cresting a hill, the violent scene being enacted in the creek below stopped

Harker's fanciful speculation dead in its tracks. Four men were laying in to one man, ragged of garb and slight of build; his thinness the result of poor nutrition.

'Another damn nester!' Collins snarled, charging down the slope, calling back, 'Come on, Harker. Time to earn those dollars I'll be putting in your pocket.'

On reaching the creek the rancher leapt from his horse and, without further ado, landed a boot in the man's ribs. Harker had to work hard to hide his fury at the cowardly act, and promised himself there and then that if for nothing else, he'd teach Collins a lesson for his brutality. Already bearing the marks of a hefty beating, the man groaned and curled up in a ball.

'Caught him stealing water from the creek, Mr Collins,' Stan Baker, the leader of the loutish quartet said. 'We were just about to string him up. Figuring that that's what you'd want, boss.'

'That's what I want, Baker,' Collins confirmed.

Bob Harker cursed the timing of his arrival. Being an agent of the law, there was no way that he could let the unfortunate nester be lynched. And were he to act, he would scupper the elaborate scheme he had thought up to bring an end to Collins's brutal hold over the valley and all who lived in it.

'There's no shortage of trees, fellas,' Baker barked. 'Pick one.'

Baker glared at Harker, making no secret of his hostility towards him. Also, Harker reckoned that Baker, fearing his position of dominance in the Broken Arrow order of things to be under threat by his hiring, was particularly keen to bolster that position by showing Collins that he would not be found wanting in carrying out his every order to the letter, irrespective of how brutal and unjust that command might be.

Baker dragged the moaning man to where one of the men had slung a rope, and was about to put the noose round his neck when Butch Collins intervened.

'Hold it, Stan. You hang him, Harker!'

'I can do it just fine, Mr Collins,' Stan Baker said waspishly.

'I know you can, Stan,' Collins said. 'But I reckon that it's about time that Mr Harker earned his living. What're you waiting for?' the rancher pressed Harker seconds later.

Bob Harker took the makings from his shirtpocket and began to roll a smoke.

'I like to have a drag before I kill a man,' he said, taking up a nonchalant pose. 'I never thought that the pleasure of seeing a man die should be rushed, Mr Collins.'

'You might have a point at that, Harker,' the rancher conceded. 'But I don't want to have to wait around. I've got a ranch to run.' He snatched the quirly from Harker's lips. 'Besides, I figure that a man should smoke on his own time. Not the time I'm paying for.'

He glanced to the pitiful nester.

'Hang him,' he ordered Harker. 'Now!'

'You're the boss,' Harker said, strolling towards the nester with casual ease.

As he approached, the nester's weeping eyes bore into Bob Harker.

'I've got a wife and two babbies, mister,' he pleaded.

'That ain't my affair,' Harker growled.

'Ain't you 'fraid that the devil will claim your soul for what you're about to do?' the nester said.

Harker laughed harshly. 'No. You see, my friend, the devil holds a marker on my soul for a long time.'

Harker could feel the burn of Collins and the other men's eyes on him, as he bent to readjust the noose and test the rope, playing for time and hoping that a miracle would happen that would allow him off the hook and make it possible for him to continue the charade that would eventually see Butch Collins hang for the evil he perpetrated.

But it seemed like the good Lord was not listening today.

'What the hell are you doing, Harker?' Collins questioned angrily.

'Only checking that the rope will do the job, Mr Collins.'

'Hang him now!' Collins roared. He drew his sixgun. 'Or I'll blast you where you stand, Harker.'

Harker had searched frantically for a way out, but he had failed to find a solution to his dilemma. Now time had run out, and his carefully laid plans were about to go up in smoke. Meaning that Butch Collins's murderous hold over Sweetwater Valley would continue until someone else could come up with a scheme to end his evil reign.

Bob Harker tensed, and readied himself for the showdown to come.

Five of them. Butch Collins, already holding a cocked Colt. Though he was fast, Harker knew that he faced impossible odds.

7

The crack of a rifle from an unseen shooter had Butch Collins and his henchmen dancing an Irish jig as bullets peppered the ground round them. Then it was Harker's turn to duck and dive as lead buzzed round him too — Ned Benton, he reckoned. It wouldn't do for him to be the exception. They mounted up and rode hell-for-leather back over the hill which Harker and Collins had crested a short time before, the saving of their own hides now more urgent than hanging the nester.

'Who the hell is shooting!' was Butch Collins's angry and frightened yell.

No one had an answer to his question except Bob Harker, and he was keeping it to himself.

As they vanished over the top of the hill, Harker glanced back and saw the nester vanishing into the wooded slopes of the creek. Having escaped a lynching, because Harker figured that he'd have died first and then the nester would have been strung up, he hoped that he'd have the good sense to quit the valley until it saw the end of Butch Collins's murderous tyranny.

The rifle fire chased them right over the brow of the hill, though by now they were out of range of serious injury. Once the safety of the other side of the hill was reached, Collins drew rein. He wiped the sheen of perspiration from his forehead.

'We was in no danger,' one of the riders boasted, in a show of bravado now that the danger had passed. 'He had a lot of lead, but he was a lousy shot.'

Butch Collins's assessment was shrewder.

'Either that, or he was a damn fine shot.'

Bob Harker held his breath. While the others would think like the man who had offered his view of the shooter's skills, Collins was a cunning and clever man who would question the fact that so many bullets could have come so close to nailing them, but had always been an inch away.

'Maybe,' Collins said, his gaze on Harker, 'the shooter was so good that he could make us dance, without making the mistake of killing any of us?'

'Yeah,' Stan Baker said. 'Come to think of it, that's exactly what he did, boss!'

'Now why would the shooter want to do that, do you think, Harker?' the rancher probed.

Harker felt that he was lumbering from one crisis to another, all designed to unmask him, and he had the feeling that he might not be favoured by the kind of luck that would be necessary to carry through his assignment. As casually as he could, he suggested:

'Maybe the nesters have hired their own protection.'

'Where would a bunch of nesters get the dollars to hire a sharp-shooter?' one of the men wondered.

'That's a real good question, Hank,' Butch Collins said, his gaze drifting Bob Harker's way.

'Maybe one of your neighbours is using the nesters to get at you, Mr Collins,' Harker suggested.

'That could make a whole lot of sense, boss,' the man called Hank said, a view that took hold.

'Could be Frank Bateman over at the Big B stirring trouble,' Stan Baker said. He fondled the sixgun on his right hip. 'Want me to pay him a visit, Mr Collins?'

'I've got a better idea,' the Broken Arrow bossman said slyly. 'Why don't you call on Bateman, Harker. Give him my regards.'

Harker chuckled. 'I guess it's about time I introduced myself to the neighbours at that. But, being a greenhorn about the geography of the valley, I'll need telling as to how I'll find the Big B.'

'Head north in a straight line for a

couple of miles,' Collins said. 'Bateman's crew will rail you in as soon as you touch Bateman grass.'

'If they don't shoot you before that,' Baker sniggered.

As he rode away, Harker ignored the laughter behind him.

★ ★ ★

As she sat on the bank of the creek where she had come to ponder, Jess Blossom's thoughts were buzzing around more wildly than a riled bee. On the ride to the creek and since, she had not been able to make any sense of her feelings. Her mind kept returning to her hectic meeting with Bob Harker, and how she had so badly misjudged the stranger to Sweetwater Valley. There had been no hint in his dashing rescue of her of his true self. Even though she had heard in vivid detail from her pa about Bob's shooting of the man in town, she still found it difficult to relate the man who had so bravely rescued her to the cold-blooded killer her pa had spoken of. And even more startling was Butch Collins's swift hiring of a man who claimed that Collins had earlier tried to lynch him. Startling but not surprising, because these days Butch was surrounding himself with the dregs of human kind. And though she had hotly rejected Bob Harker's claim that Butch had tried to hang him, she had heard scraps of other stories about Broken Arrow range law. Her difficulty in getting a more comprehensive view of those stories was that every time she put in an appearance when one of those stories was being told, mouths shut.

Her pa was forthright and consistent in his condemnation of Butch Collins.

'He's a viper that one day soon will be stepped on, Jess,' he'd told her. 'And if you marry him, my door will be closed to you.'

Were her sudden doubts about her future happiness as Butch Collins' wife, brought about because being cut off from her pa would break her heart? Or was there another reason?

Bob Harker!

But how could she possibly have any feelings for a cold-blooded killer? And was it possible to fall in love with a man whom she had only just met?

'Oh, Jess Blossom,' she groaned. 'You're in a darn awful muddle, girl!'

★ ★ ★

'That's far enough!'

The steely command ringing clarion-clear from a stand of pine to his right, and the sound of a bullet slotting into the breach of a rifle, brought Bob Harker up short.

'This is Bateman range. Who are you? State your business,' the unseen man commanded. The staccato enquiry had a no-nonsense quality.

'The name's Harker. I'm an emissary from the Broken Arrow.'

'What business would that bastard Collins have with a Bateman?' the man wanted to know.

'Are you Frank Bateman?' Harker asked the man in the trees.

The man emerged from cover, Winchester pointed at Harker.

'I'm a Bateman. Jack Bateman, Frank Bateman's nephew. What's this business you've come about?'

'What I've got to say is for Frank Bateman's ears alone.'

As Jack Bateman drew closer, Bob Harker had a feeling of having seen the man somewhere before.

'My uncle doesn't see many people these days, Harker. Say what you've come to say and leave.' He raised the rifle a significant inch. 'Triggers in this valley can be real jumpy.'

Harker shunned compromise.

'Like I said, it's Frank Bateman I've come to see. Not a second-stringer.'

Jack Bateman stiffened.

'You're real lippy for a man under the threat of a rifle, mister. Now that makes you one of two things. Very brave. Or very stupid.'

He waved the rifle to indicate to

Harker that he should ride ahead.

'Take it slow and easy,' he warned. 'Or I'll cut you down like a damn weed in good grass.'

'Nothing like a Bateman welcome,' Harker snorted.

*   *   *

Her worries unresolved, Jess Blossom returned to town with a heavy heart. As she passed the law office, Bart Rattigan was stepping out.

'Howdy, Jess,' he greeted.

'Hello, Sheriff Rattigan,' Jess said, and on impulse asked: 'Did Bob Harker really shoot that man down in cold blood today, like everyone says, Mr Rattigan?'

'Well, to be fair to Harker, Lacey did make all the running.'

Jesses relief was short-lived.

'But I guess that's what Harker did all right, shoot Lacey down in cold blood.'

'But if Lacey made all the running as

you say, Sheriff,' Jess said desperately.

'Thing is, Jess, that if he'd wanted to, Harker could have as easily winged Lacey as kill him.' He shook his head. 'Because Lacey wasn't anyway near as gun-handy or as fast as Harker.'

'Then why didn't you throw Bob Harker in jail?' Jess demanded to know.

'Because when it came down to it, as I said, Lacey made all the running.'

Jess Blossom rode on, heavy-hearted.

★ ★ ★

'Along the hall to the room at the end,' Jack Bateman instructed Harker, and marched behind him, the rifle a whisper away from his spine.

At the end of the hall Jack Bateman danced ahead of Harker and knocked on a solid mahogany door, strong enough to withstand cannon fire.

'Company from the Broken Arrow, Uncle Frank,' he announced, easing open the den door.

Stepping into the den, Bob Harker

froze on seeing the man in the invalid chair, because he knew him and what he had been before he had become a rancher. And the question was:

Would Frank Bateman remember him?

8

Bob Harker's mind went back to when he had been a Pinkerton detective, before he became a special agent for the governor's office. Frank Bateman, then a man ten years younger and a whole lot fitter than the man he was now looking at, had assigned him his first Pinkerton investigation. It had not been the kind of assignment that made headlines or that anyone would remember, merely an investigation of small amounts of cash being purloined from a mining company. But he recalled that back then, Frank Bateman's boast was that he never forgot a face. Could the cripple before him now still boast of that? If he could, then he'd recall him, and that he had resigned to enrol in the new élite team of special governor's agents.

He had spent two years as a

Pinkerton, and that meant that it was eight years since Frank Bateman had last set eyes on him. It also explained the sense of familiarity he had had on seeing Jack Bateman, because Frank Bateman's nephew had more than a passing resemblance to the younger and fitter man who used to be a Pinkerton.

Harker recalled how Bateman had often spoken of one day turning to ranching, a dream he had obviously fulfilled, but it would seem at a great personal cost. He wondered how Bateman had ended up in an invalid chair. He did not reckon on a stroke, the normal route to an invalid chair, because Frank Bateman's eyes were still button-bright with alertness and intelligence. So that suggested that his invalidity stemmed from physical injury rather than cerebral incapacity.

As the invalid chair rolled towards him, Bob Harker struck a bold pose, seeing no point in timidity. Bateman would recognize him or he would not, it was as simple as that. If he recognized him, all he could do was take him into his confidence and hope that he respected that confidence. The thing was that the turmoil in Sweetwater Valley, though in the main believed to be the work of Butch Collins, might also involve others, like Frank Bateman.

As a Pinkerton, Frank Bateman had been arrow-straight. But he had seen honest men go bad before when they pursued their dreams or were corrupted by greed.

The question was, had the Bateman ranch been built on sweat and hard labour? Or by the easier route of tough-arm tactics? Was Frank Bateman still the man he had known? Or had he become another Butch Collins?

'For a Broken Arrow hardcase you got pretty far,' Frank Bateman growled. He glanced at his nephew. 'You're lucky that my nephew asks questions before he starts shooting.' And then a touch critically, he added, 'I keep telling him that it's a flaw that will one day get him killed in this murderous valley.'

By now Frank Bateman had rolled up to Harker's toecaps, and his study of him was intense.

'New to the valley?' he enquired of Harker.

'Yeah.'

Jack Bateman snorted. 'Butch Collins's latest gunslinger, I reckon, Uncle Frank.'

Frank Bateman rolled back a little and let his gaze run over Bob Harker.

'He's got the gait, sure enough, Jack,' was his conclusion about his nephew's assertion. 'So what're you doing on Bateman range, mister?'

Harker relaxed a little, but not completely. Frank Bateman had taken a good look at him and had not, as far as he could tell, recognized him. But then, remembering Bateman's Pinkerton days, the rancher was a better actor than most, and could keep his thoughts firmly inside his skull without them showing on his face, until he was good and ready to let them show.

He could still have recognized him,

and be playing him for his own purposes until he was ready to spring the trap he might be baiting.

'A short while ago Mr Collins had occasion to take to task a nester on his range.' Harker grinned, scoffingly. 'The boss was about to deal out the *usual* punishment for such impertinence, when a sharp-shooter intervened.'

'Did he kill Collins by any chance?' was Frank Bateman's hopeful question.

Harker shook his head.

'Too bad! The valley would be well rid of a skunk.'

'I'll tell Mr Collins your opinion of him,' Harker drawled.

'No need. He already knows.'

'What's Collins's problem got to do with us?' Jack Bateman queried.

'Well, you see, the bossman thought at first that the nesters might have hired themselves a sharp-shooter. But then where would a crowd of penniless hobos find the kind of money it would take to pay such a man?'

Bob Harker settled fierce eyes on

Frank Bateman.

'So Mr Collins dismissed the idea of the nesters hiring the sharp-shooter. And when he did that, his mind turned to neighbours who would have the kind of money needed to hire such help. If you get my drift, Bateman?'

If Frank Bateman could have gotten out of his invalid chair, Harker reckoned that he'd have taken quite a bashing from the furious rancher.

'I do my own fighting!' he roared. 'I don't need to hire in rats like you, mister! And nesters 've got rights, too. This is free government land. Boundaries are yet to be decided. This is a big valley. There's land for every man, cowman and sodbuster.'

Harker hated his cruelty, but his purpose was to establish himself as a genuine Broken Arrow no-good.

'Seems to me,' he began, fixing his stare on Frank Bateman's thin, shrivelled legs, 'that swatting a fly would be too much for you, Bateman.'

'Get out of my house,' Frank

Bateman bellowed. 'And if you come back, the next time you'll stay put. Buried right where a Bateman gun will drop you.'

Bob Harker slouched in an impudent pose.

'The next time I come a-calling, Bateman. I might not be of such an amenable frame of mind.'

'You heard my uncle.' Jack Bateman's rifle prodded Harker between the shoulders. 'Git!'

Harker turned his head.

'I don't like being prodded, mister. Don't forget being prodded either.'

'To hell with you,' Jack Bateman snarled.

'That's a real probability,' Harker agreed. 'The thing is, you might get there before me, should you have an accident.'

Harker turned and swaggered out of the room.

'Be seeing you gents,' he flung back.

'You keep in mind what I said,' Frank Bateman warned. 'The next time you set foot on Bateman grass, it'll be your last time doing anything this side of hell.'

Bob Harker laughed dismissively.

'Cripples shouldn't threaten. That invalid chair just might roll off a ridge or topple into a well.' He paused in the doorway. 'Any message for Mr Collins, Bateman?'

'From now on, any message for Butch Collins will be inside a bullet,' Jack Bateman barked.

Bob Harker chuckled. 'Now if I tell the boss that, nephew, he might get real mad and ride over here to run you folk right out of the valley.'

'Let him come,' Frank Bateman said sombrely.

Harker shrugged and left.

Riding away from the Bateman ranch house, he was full of self-loathing. He knew that he was simply playing a role, but it was alien to his nature to be so offensive to any man. And he would not blame Frank Bateman one iota if, in his fury, he cut him down for the heartless and cruel critter he posed as.

At least he had had the wisdom to have used an alias for his assignment. If his own name of Lar Blaney was in the public domain, Frank Bateman would have recognized him instantly.

As he rode across Bateman range, he could feel the burn of watching eyes on him. Now and then a man showed himself to egg him on his way. The air in the valley crackled with tension, and Harker figured that he had little time to prevent an all-out range war and the death and destruction that such a bitter feud would bring. The temptation was to throw caution to the wind. However, any impetuousness on his part could scupper his scheme to see Butch Collins behind bars, and likely on a gallows. And removing him from the valley was, that he could see, the only sure way of bringing calm and restoring peace.

He wondered how Frank Bateman had been imprisoned in an invalid chair? After their brief but fiery exchange, Harker was convinced that Bateman, the man, was light years away from Butch Collins. In fact he was certain that the former Pinkerton detective was the kind of fairminded and honest man that Sweetwater Valley needed, and under whose guidance it would thrive.

Harker recalled Frank Bateman's spirited defence of the nesters, and his generous nature in believing that there was land enough for all men in the valley.

Being ridden easy and not expecting the volley of shots that buzzed round him, his horse was spooked and he had to fight to control the mare. Laughter came from behind a nearby hillock. Harker ignored the laughter, considering it a little light relief in an atmosphere that was rife with foreboding. As he controlled the mare, he reckoned that he was now on Broken Arrow range, and that the volley of shots had marked his departure from Bateman grass.

From out of nowhere another volley of shots rang out. One of the men behind the hillock jumped up clutching at his back, and toppled over, face down. A second man ran for the cover of nearby trees, but did not make it. And, judging by the intensity of the gunfire that brought him down, Bob Harker reckoned that he must have a hole in every inch of his body.

Stan Baker and Bengy Smallwood, leading a string of Broken Arrow hardcases made an appearance from where they had been lying in ambush, sharing raucous laughter at the unfortunate men's demise.

Harker sighed.

'I'm never going to keep a lid on this damn powderkeg of a valley!' he groaned.

9

'I've been racking my brains to figure out where I saw this fella Harker before, Bart,' Frank Bateman said to his dinner-guest that evening.

'Probably nowhere,' Sheriff Bart Rattigan said. 'Harker's got the kind of face that fits under most hats, Frank.'

Bateman shook his head vehemently.

'I just know we've crossed paths before, Bart,' he stated emphatically. 'And sooner or later I'll remember where.'

'Harker being a hardcase, and you having been a Pinkerton man, your paths likely crossed in the course of Pinkerton business,' the sheriff speculated.

'Probably,' Bateman agreed.

Rattigan grinned. 'While you're trying to recall,' he held out his glass, 'I'll sip some more of that Kentucky rye.' When

Bateman had poured a generous drink into the sheriff's elegant crystal tumbler, he said: 'Trouble today. Two men dead, I hear.'

Frank Bateman frowned. 'Two good men at that. Ben Leary and Walt Crocker. Shot down in cold blood.'

'Collins's outfit?'

'Who else,' the rancher snapped, and asked, a tad critical: 'When're you going to march that cur to the gallows, Bart?'

'You can't march a man anywhere until you get the evidence to present to a judge and jury, Frank,' was Bart Rattigan's starchy reply.

Frank Bateman scoffed. 'You're never going to get a jury to try Butch Collins round these parts, Bart. Those he can't buy off, he'll scare off.'

The sheriff sighed. 'There rests the kernel of the problem, Frank.'

'You know, Harker's visit today was as a result of a sharp-shooter's interrupting Collins's favourite sport of lynching nesters. And maybe the idea of hiring our own gun-slick ain't such a bad idea after all.'

Rattigan sat bolt upright in his chair.

'Do that, Frank, and you'd be no better than Collins,' he rebuked Bateman. 'And I'd show no favour,' he warned.

'That's what it's coming to, Bart.' Frank Bateman slammed his fist on the dinner-table. 'It's that or roll over and hand the valley to Butch Collins. I was thinking that maybe we could persuade Harker, with the right inducement, to switch sides. What d'ya say, Bart?'

'I've already told you,' Rattigan said, his mood uncompromising, 'you go down that road and I'll treat you no diff'rent from Collins, Frank.'

'Aw, shut up and eat your dinner,' Bateman growled, good-naturedly. 'I ain't got any intention of aping Broken Arrow tactics.'

Bart Rattigan eyed his old friend keenly.

'I ain't,' Bateman reassured the Hett's Landing lawman.

However, Rattigan had an uneasy

feeling. Of all the spreads in the valley, the Bateman ranch had suffered Butch Collins's spite the most, because to extend his boundaries it would be necessary for Collins to remove the first and major obstacle to his progress, and that was the Bateman ranch. And the sheriff also knew that when push came to shove, Frank Bateman would fight.

The feuding in Sweetwater Valley had been going on for most of two years now, getting progressively dirtier as Collins prodded more and more. Rattigan knew that patience and tolerance would not last for ever, in fact not much longer, he reckoned. Sooner rather than later, Sweetwater Valley would be involved in a no-holds-barred range war, and there was not much he could do to stop it without the help of a US marshal. Or better still, one of those tough-as-nails governor's agents he'd heard about.

He had presided over several fiery meetings in the valley of late. Like Frank Bateman, his neighbours' patience was running out. That Bateman had raised the idea of luring Harker away from the Broken Arrow was worrying. It was the seed of a notion that could quickly grow to a full-blown proposal, especially if Bateman were to raise such a possibility at one of those increasingly bad-tempered ranchers' meetings.

And if it was not Harker, then it would be some equally unprincipled bastard who would take up their offer. It was hard to blame the ranchers, Rattigan admitted in the confines of his own thoughts. His reaction, were he continuously pestered by mysterious fires, poisoned water-holes and dead stock, might not be any different.

In fact it could be a lot more hostile.

But if hostilities broke out, there could be no doubting the outcome. Collins had a small army of men willing to do anything for a dollar; men who were gun-handy. In the main, they would be taking on men who used their guns infrequently, using them mostly as a tool to hammer nails more often than for their proper purpose. In fact most of the ranchers' shooting would probably be a mile wide of the side of a barn.

'Heard you ordered Baker and Smallwood out of the territory, Bart, that right?' Bateman's question derailed Bart Rattigan's dreary thoughts. 'They ain't left. Jack saw the pair today over on the south pasture of the Broken Arrow, large as life. Are you aiming to run them out?' Bateman asked in a no-frills fashion. 'If you don't, having said so, that pair will wag your tail, Bart.'

'Tell me something I don't know, Frank,' Rattigan said wearily.

'More roast beef?'

The sheriff shook his head. 'The appetite's gone right off me.'

* * *

Butch Collins looked up from the accounts book he was working on when Bob Harker entered the den.

'Well,' he barked, 'did you throw a

scare into that stinking old cripple Bateman?'

'I reckon he was a little jittery when I left,' Harker opined.

'A *little jittery*,' he mocked. 'You should have scared the hell out of him.'

'I don't reckon that he scares that easy, Mr Collins.'

The rancher studied Harker.

'You know, there's something not quite right about you, Harker,' he declared. 'For a man who shot down Jeb Lacey in cold blood, you seem to blow hot and cold when it comes to dealing with an old bastard like Frank Bateman.'

His scrutiny of Harker intensified. 'Now, I wonder why that is?'

'All you asked was that I'd throw a scare into Bateman. If you wanted me to . . . shall we say, be a little more aggressive, then you should have said so.'

'Don't give me lip, Harker,' the rancher roared, springing furiously out of his chair. 'For two bits I'd have you horsewhipped.'

Harker became properly remorseful.

'Didn't intend any offence, Mr Collins. Now if you want me to do whatever you want with Bateman, then that's what I'll do.'

The governor's agent held his breath. Would Collins take the bait and order him to kill Frank Bateman? If he did, he could immediately arrest him and sling him in jail, and he would be removed from the valley for the greater good. But that would not be the same as getting him for murder as such. He could always recant and say that he had spoken in jest, and it would be impossible to prove otherwise. His absence from Sweetwater Valley would only be a temporary respite from mayhem. And there was the difficulty of his word against the powerful rancher's. Any half-baked attorney would have it thrown out of court in a flash. His strategy was a risky but necessary one. To worm his way into his confidence, he had to convince Butch Collins that he would do his bidding. Because only if he succeeded in achieving this would he have a chance of getting the evidence which would nail Collins good and proper.

'You'd kill him, if I said so?' Collins asked.

'You pay the piper, Mr Collins.'

Butch Collins relaxed and sat down. 'Whiskey?'

'Don't mind if I do.'

Collins nodded in the direction of a drinks cabinet. 'Pour two.'

'My pleasure,' Harker said, strolling to the drinks cabinet with an easy lope.

'Sit down, Harker,' the rancher said, when he returned with the drinks. When Harker was seated, Collins continued: 'You know, sometimes the burden of building a ranch can make a man real weary.'

'I guess,' Harker said, curious as to what direction Butch Collins's confidence was going to take, and careful to maintain an air of interest to encourage the rancher to elaborate, while at the same time not seeming too eager to pry.

Collins considered Harker for a long spell before going on:

'It would be a help if a man could share his troubles with a trusted ally.'

'I guess,' Harker said again. 'There's always Jess Blossom to talk to,' he suggested. Butch Collins snorted.

'A woman is for pleasure and cooking.'

Bob Harker forced down the urge to leap off the sofa he was seated on, yank the rancher out of his chair and thrash him. What in tarnation was Jess getting herself into, marrying a man who would see his wife in such a menial role.

'Jess, I figure, is a mighty intelligent woman,' he said.

Collins's eyes narrowed in an intense scrutiny of Harker. When he chuckled, there was about as much mirth in his laughter as there was in a snake-bite.

'Stan Baker says that you and Jess seemed real friendly after you rescued her from that accident you caused.'

'Me?' Harker exclaimed good-humouredly. 'I'd say that Jess played her part in it, hogging the middle of the road the way she was.'

Butch Collins dropped his mask of geniality.

'Jess Blossom is off-bounds, Harker. To you or any other man,' he added menacingly.

Bob Harker spread himself on the couch expansively.

'Jess ain't my kinda gal, boss,' he said. 'I like my women to be . . . ' He rolled his eyes to heaven seeking inspiration, 'well, less saintly and more devilish.'

Butch Collins burst into laughter.

'Me, too, Harker.'

Harker's brow furrowed. 'Then how come you're marrying Jess Blossom?'

'Simple. I've got big plans. And a man with ambition needs a wife that he can trot out in public.' He winked slyly. 'A man can always express his earthier side in other places.'

Bob Harker thought: he's an even bigger sidewinder than I imagined!

'You're a smart man, Mr Collins,'

Harker complimented, fighting more than ever his urge to lay into him.

'I'm thinking that you're no dimwit yourself, Harker.' Collins paused. 'Like to hear how I built the Broken Arrow? And how I intend to make it the biggest ranch in the territory?'

'That I'd find a mighty interesting story, Mr Collins,' Harker said, counting a beat.

'Pour us a couple more whiskeys,' the rancher said generously, obviously confident that in Harker he had found a man with whom he could boast about his past and intended future misdeeds.

As Harker poured the drinks, his back turned to the rancher, he wished he could give free rein to his delight at having achieved so swiftly what he had counted on weeks or months to acquire.

Butch Collins's black-hearted and bloody history.

★ ★ ★

'I guess it's normal for a woman about to get married to be off her food,' Art Blossom observed, as Jess used her fork to move her uneaten meal aimlessly round her plate. 'But I'm thinking that it's the problems rather than the joys that's got you so preoccupied, Jess.'

'Problems?' Jess hedged.

'I've known you since the cradle, Jess. You can't fool your old pa. Now tell me what's troubling you enough to put you off your food.'

Jess was about to continue hedging, but Art Blossom was not buying.

'For some strange and silly reason, tying the knot with Butch Collins isn't as attractive an idea as it was,' Jess confessed.

'Might I ask when this doubt took hold?'

Jess shrugged.

'Maybe when Harker put in an appearance?' he suggested shrewdly.

'That's a real silly notion, Pa,' she said scoffingly. 'Bob Harker is a gunfighter.'

'And Butch Collins is the man who hired his skills,' Blossom pointedly reminded his daughter. 'That, to my way of thinking, puts Collins in the same barrel of rotten apples.'

Jess Blossom sprang up from the table.

'Can't you ever see any good in Butch?' she wailed.

'No,' Blossom stated bluntly.

'Oh . . . ' Jess Blossom's fingers agitated her blond hair. 'You're impossible, Pa!'

She flounced around the room like a blind woman trying to find the way out. Blossom waited patiently until his daughter's angry energy was used up. When she eventually flung herself back on to her chair, he said:

'I figure that you should forget both men, Jess.'

'Both?'

'Sure. It's obvious to me, and probably to everyone else who was watching on the street today, that you were mightily disappointed when Harker signed on as a Broken Arrow man. My guess is that you had seen him in a kinder light. In fact, speaking bluntly, as the man who had replaced Butch Collins in your affections, Jess.'

Jess sprang off her chair again.

'Pa, sometimes you talk the most nonsensical rubbish!' she declared.

'And sometimes, just like your ma, rest her soul, you can be as deaf as a stone to the truth. Like every time she pampered that no-good cousin of hers from Utah, despite my telling her that he'd never amount to anything more than the conniving cur he was born as.'

Jess Blossom stopped dead in her tracks.

'So that's why you don't like anyone from Utah.'

'Your ma's cousin never gave me any reason to like anyone from Utah!'

'Well, all I can say is that if Ma was as deaf as a stone you're as stubborn as a mule, Pa.'

'Fiddly!'

A long, tension-crackling impasse

ensued, and held until Art's and Jess Blossom's steam evaporated. Then Jess asked:

'What am I to do, Pa? I'm more addled than a doddering ninety-year-old. And don't tell me to forget both Butch and Bob,' she pleaded. 'Because that's not going to happen.'

'At least postpone the wedding,' he said, after due deliberation. Jess was shocked. 'It will give you time to think, gal,' he added sagely.

Jess Blossom bit her lower lip. 'And what if Butch decides to look elsewhere for a wife?'

Blossom snorted. 'You'd have suffered no loss, Jess.'

'I don't want to be left on the shelf, Pa.'

'Better than ending up in the dog-house, I say.'

'Dog-house?' Jess laughed. 'Butch would be good to me.'

'Maybe. But only if you're willing to be his damn doormat.'

'Doormat! I'd be his wife and partner.'

'Doormat,' Art Blossom insisted.

'And what would I be if I married Bob Harker?'

'Not a doormat, I reckon. You'd be much too busy dodging the law with him.' Blossom took his daughter in his arms. 'There's lots of good men who'd be more than pleased to have you in their house, Jess.'

'If I don't get married now, Pa, no man that I know of would want me near him. Who'd want a woman who's almost reached the altar twice?'

Art Blossom knew the veracity of his daughter's claim.

'Well, better a happy old maid than a tormented wife, I say,' he opined.

'But I don't want to be an old maid!' Jess wailed.

10

Butch Collins slugged deeply from his fourth whiskey. An hour had gone by. Collins had talked a lot, but in essence had said nothing; at least nothing specific enough for Harker to consider as evidence. The rancher's rambling diatribe was more a listing of his own self-worth, than a confession of his misdeeds, and all the time he was getting more inebriated. Soon, he'd pass out, and Harker would have wasted his time.

The rancher proffered his glass.

'Fill it up again,' he ordered Harker. 'And pour for yourself, too.'

Harker considered a rebuke to try and stem the rancher's drinking, but decided against it. He'd come across as a moralist, and that would not be in keeping with a man whom Collins now considered to be a soulmate. He had no choice but to go along.

Taking his own empty glass, the liquor having been surreptitiously disposed of by Harker into a cactus-plant alongside the sofa (it would be the drunkest cactus in all of the West), he went to the drinks cabinet to open a second bottle of Kentucky Rye. It was a fine brew that brought a warm glow to a man's innards. Normally, Harker would have no objection to matching the rancher drop for drop, but he had to remain lucid and sober, in case Butch Collins spilled the beans he was hoping he'd spill. But the prospect of his doing so was fast disappearing. Like all drunks, he'd progress ever deeper into maudlin.

Harker returned with the drinks and handed Collins his, of which he instantly gulped half. Despondent, Bob Harker sat on the sofa, immediately emptying three quarters of the rye in his glass into the cactus. The thing will start singing shortly, he mused. Butch Collins slumped in his chair. At least, thankfully, it would be over soon.

Harker waited until the rancher's eyelids drooped and his breathing became ragged. He went to leave and was at the door when, as drunks do before sliding into oblivion, Collins revived momentarily.

'Shot that old bastard Bateman in the spine!'

Butch Collins laughed, a frightening insanity sparkled in his eyes. Then with a heavy sigh, like a dying man, he collapsed into a whiskey-induced stupor. Maybe, Bob Harker thought, it would be better for everyone if Collins just kept sliding into the black hole he had dropped into and never came back.

★   ★   ★

'You know, I've had better company in my time,' Bart Rattigan said. 'Just as well I've got a good whiskey.'

Frank Bateman came back from the reverie he had slipped into for the umpteenth time during dinner and even more so since the sheriff and he had sought the comfort of the log-fire in the sitting-room.

'Sorry, Bart,' he apologized. 'I reckon that I'm the worst company a man could have around tonight.'

'Are you still trying to figure out where you've seen Harker before?' Rattigan asked, shaking his head in wonder at what he obviously considered to be a useless exercise. 'Just as well you're grey. Because if you weren't at the start of dinner, you'd certainly be by now,' he observed amusedly.

'There ain't a dodger on him by any chance?'

The sheriff of Hett's Landing shook his head.

'First thing I checked out.'

'Don't you reckon there should be, if Harker is the killer he's supposed to be, Bart?'

Bart Rattigan became thoughtful.

'Well, now that you mention it, Frank. I guess it is kinda strange at that.'

Bateman grunted. 'Mighty strange, if you ask me.'

Bart Rattigan's thoughts were set on a new track by Bateman's prompting.

'Maybe,' the rancher continued, 'it might be a good idea to check out Harker a little more, Bart.'

The Hett's Landing sheriff agreed.

'I'll do that first thing tomorrow, Frank,' he promised.

★ ★ ★

Leaving the Collins ranch house, Harker mounted up and made a pretence, for any watcher's benefit, of setting trail for town. However, once out of sight, and as sure as he could be that he had not been followed, he switched trails and rode into the hills to the prearranged meeting-place with Jeb Lacey and Ned Benton to bring them up to date with developments. Conscious of Frank Bateman's talent for remembering faces, he felt that it was only a matter of time before Bateman would place his. Knowing Bateman, if he had the slightest inkling of having known him, he would not let go. The change of name from Lar Blaney to Bob Harker might throw him for a spell, but not for long.

Luck, Harker had always known, would be a vital factor if his plan to undo Butch Collins were to succeed. And that luck deserted him when, a mile or so from the shack in the hills he was headed for, Stan Baker, ambling back to the Broken Arrow from a visit to a local woman of an accommodating nature, spotted a shadowy rider on the hill trail, so close in fact that, had there not been a stout tree to slip behind, they would have ridden into each other.

At first Baker thought it was an interloper of one sort or another, and was about to grab his rifle and cut him down. But there was something familiar about the rider, so he decided to track him. And being a man used to stealth, Bob Harker rode on, unaware of having picked up a follower.

A short distance on, as the moon broke through the clouds which had covered the valley most of the day, the stalker could see Harker clearly.

'Well, my oh my,' Baker murmured. 'Now I wonder what Mr Harker is doing wandering about in the hills at dead of night?'

11

Jeb Lacey, an anxious man at the best of times, paced the abandoned shack where he and Ned Benton were hiding out. Lacey, due to the fact that he was supposed to have been killed by Harker, was compelled to stay indoors, and was beginning to show signs of cabin fever. Ned Benton secretly reconnoitred the Bateman and Collins ranges for signs of mischief, the Big B and the Broken Arrow being the main protagonists in the Sweetwater Valley feud. The common wisdom was that if Butch Collins's skulduggery had any chance of being stopped in its tracks, then Frank Bateman's was the only outfit with the clout to stop him. Collins also knew this to be the case. The success or failure of his quest to drive out his neighbours and grab the entire valley would depend on first driving Frank Bateman and his nephew out. Up to now there had been plenty of skirmishes, lost or won on about an even basis. However, everyone knew that outright range war would sooner or later decide the outcome of the opposing forces, and the fate of the valley.

So far, Bateman had resisted the call to bring in hired guns to match those Butch Collins had on his payroll. But it was coming near to the time when he would have to, if he wanted to have any chance of stopping the aggressive resetting of Broken Arrow boundaries. Frank Bateman had already lost acreage to Collins; not the best land, and probably not worth killing for, Bateman had decided. It would revert to the Big B when Collins was finished in the valley. But its loss, and what he saw as his uncle's back-sliding in facing up to Butch Collins, had dangerously raised Jack Bateman's hackles and had left the senior Bateman with the task of keeping his nephew on a tight rein while waiting for what he would consider to be the right time to take on Collins.

'You're wearing that floor so much, Jeb,' Ned Benton, the easier-going agent said, 'that you'll fall clean through it.'

Lacey, annoyed by what he thought was Benton's too relaxed approach to the job in hand, went to the window to check again the terrain outside. Seeing no sign of Bob Harker, he checked his pocket-watch for the hundredth time in as many seconds.

'The hands can barely have moved since you last checked,' Benton said, unwisely.

'Lar should have been here almost an hour ago,' barked Lacey, using Harker's real first name. 'Doesn't that worry you?'

'I reckon that he's been delayed, that's all.'

'Lar Blaney is a very prompt man, Ned.'

'Well, this is a situation that perfect timing can't be applied to, I figure.'

'Maybe Collins put two and two together when you chased him with lead today?' Lacey fretted. 'Maybe he figured that Lar's being saved from hanging that nester was a mite too convenient?'

Ned Benton worried about that also.

'There was nothing else I could do,' he reasoned. 'If I had not acted, Lar's plan would be done for, and he'd be done for, too. Because he'd have to show his hand. There was no way he could have hanged the nester, or allowed anyone else to do so either.'

Jeb Lacey, a consistent and continual worrier, was about to dwell further on the possible outcome of Benton's intervention, when he saw a rider come from the trees into the clearing in front of the shack.

'It's Lar,' he announced, relieved. He hurried to the door to open it. 'Howdy, Lar. We feared for your safety.'

'Don't call me Lar!' Harker rebuked Lacey. He dismounted. 'That was my direct order, Jeb.'

149

'What does it matter out here?' Lacey protested.

Harker relaxed. 'I guess not much, Jeb.'

Stan Baker was stunned on seeing Jeb Lacey.

'Pretty healthy for a dead man,' he murmured, on mastering his shock. And Lacey had addressed Harker as Lar, which he was not supposed to have done. So what was Harker's real name? And more important, who was he and why the need for subterfuge?

Watching the men go inside with a third man who had come to the door, Stan Baker murmured, in response to Harker's last comment: 'Now, I wouldn't exactly say that.' His tone became sarcastic, 'Lar.'

He grinned wolfishly.

'But I'm sure that Butch Collins will be very interested when I tell him that you're not who you say you are, mister.'

12

Stan Baker waited until the men were settled down in the shack before he left, walking his horse a distance away from the shack to avoid any risk of disturbing the shale on the hill trail. In the stillness of the night a dislodgement of shale would sound like rolling thunder. A tree-branch he got entangled with rustled. He waited a breath to see if Harker and his partners had been alerted. With no sign of their having heard anything, he slipped away into the night.

When well away from the shack he mounted up. A full moon coming from behind a bank of cloud lit his trail and the open range ahead. He'd make swift progress to the Broken Arrow. And if Butch Collins showed urgency, there was a chance that Harker and his cohorts could be trapped in their lair.

As Baker saw it, Harker had to be one of two things, a lawman, or maybe a detective hired by the other ranchers to gather evidence against Collins. But personally, based on Harker's fast draw, he'd opt for him being a lawman. Maybe even one of these territorial governor's agents he had heard tell of. Tough *hombres* who nailed men like Butch Collins.

Bringing news of Harker's treachery should enhance his standing with Butch Collins, and pave the way for him to share in the rich pickings that would be on offer when Collins finally decided to run his neighbours out of the valley.

Reaching open range and riding full out, Baker had dreams of easy times ahead after the feuding guns stopped blasting.

* * *

'You sure you won't stay the night, Bart?' Frank Bateman asked the Hett's Landing sheriff.

'Thanks for the invite, Frank,' Rattigan said. 'But I want to start enquiries about Harker first thing.'

'A good sleep and a fine breakfast would soak up that whiskey sloshing around in your belly. Wouldn't want you falling off your horse and breaking your neck.'

Chuckling, Rattigan swung into the saddle.

'You weren't all that free with your liquor, you old buzzard,' he joked.

'You take care, Bart,' the rancher cautioned. 'These are dangerous times.'

Riding away, the sheriff called back: 'If you think of where you saw Harker before, let me know.'

★　★　★

'What is it, Ned?' Bob Harker asked.

'Douse the light!' Benton said urgently. Harker acted instantly, then hurried to join Benton at the shack window, his keen eyes scanning the moonlit clearing in front of the shack and the terrain beyond. 'Thought I heard something, Lar,' Benton added doubtfully. 'Must be jitters, I guess.'

Jeb Lacey relaxed a little. However, Bob Harker got more tense. There was a time or two on his way to the shack that he'd had a feeling of being followed. But, as far as he could see, he had not been, and he had put his feeling down to imagination. If he had been followed, his tracker had moved like a ghost — a man used to stealth, a man like Stan Baker or Bengy Smallwood, men versed in moving quietly by the nature of their professions. Were it the case that Baker or Smallwood had tracked him, they would now be racing to the Broken Arrow to inform Butch Collins of the nocturnal shenanigans of his latest addition to the payroll. And if he had been followed, his tracker would have seen Jeb Lacey alive and kicking, and know of his sleight of hand in town.

He saw no point in worrying Lacey or Benton with his suspicions. Neither did he tell them of his visit to Frank Bateman and the danger that that visit might bring. Maybe he should call again on Bateman, reveal who and what he was, and ask for the confidence to be kept. But if he had not confided in Bart Rattigan because of the way it might shape his thinking, exactly the same applied to Bateman. His mission had to remain one of secrecy. Because there had been Broken Arrrow men killed as well, and he had to be even handed and open minded. It was probable that Frank Bateman's actions were strictly above board, but he was confined to an invalid chair, and Jack Bateman might be involved in mayhem he did not know about or would not countenance.

'I guess we should get this meeting over with, Lar,' Lacey suggested.

That was another worry. His tracker, if he had had one, would probably have heard Lacey call him by his real name when he had arrived. Without his surname, there might not be any great risk of his true identity being known.

But things had a way of adding up.

'If you're missed back at the Broken Arrow, it'll raise questions,' Lacey said.

'Jeb's got a good point there, Lar,' Ned Benton agreed. 'You shouldn't be missing for too long.'

It was with a sense of the clock running against him, that Harker resumed the meeting.

13

His mood mellowed by Frank Bateman's Kentucky rye, Bart Rattigan was enjoying the moonlit ride back to town, letting the mare set her own pace, while he dreamed about quitting the troubles of the sheriff's office in the not too distant future, and pondering on what life would be like back East with his brother and how, after a lifetime of Western living, he'd take to paved streets, well-kept parks and the rainier climate of Boston. After due deliberation he concluded that any place where there were no cows or range and the hot lead that went with them, he'd find mighty pleasing.

So deep in thought was he that he almost missed sight of the fast-moving rider eating up the trail coming towards him. Living in troubled country, a fast rider usually meant only one thing, more trouble. Instinctively, he eased off to the side of the trail near a bend. By the way the rider kept coming apace, Rattigan figured that he was on an errand of great urgency, or he was fleeing a crime, the latter being the more likely, because his direction suggested that his ultimate destination was the Broken Arrow.

He waited, listening to the rider draw near, ready to pounce.

★   ★   ★

Jess Blossom woke from a restless dream, just as Bob Harker's lips were about to meet hers. She sat up in bed, flustered and feeling guilty, and unsure of what the dream meant. Should she not have dreamed of Butch Collins, her probable future husband, instead of Bob Harker, a man she hardly knew.

Restless and unable to get back to sleep, Jess went downstairs to sit in the parlour to finish reading a book about a big house on an English moor where all sorts of mystery and intrigue took place. Reading-matter in Hett's Landing normally consisted of dime novels of poor quality and even poorer content. Fortunately, Art Blossom, a book-reading man, had gone to great lengths to fill the bookshelves in the parlour with a wide variety of books of which her preference was for English authors. She revelled in the atmosphere of windswept moors and foggy London streets and country houses where all sorts of mystery, murder and mayhem abounded. Dark brooding heroes and ghostly wails in the night. And heroines who overcame impossible odds to win the man they loved. She had only just opened the book when the parlour door opened and Art Blossom entered the room.

'Did I wake you, Pa?' Jess queried regretfully. 'I thought I came downstairs like a ghost.'

'You did,' he comfirmed. 'The fact is that I haven't had a wink tonight.'

'What's troubling you?' Jess asked, concerned.

'Your happiness, Jess,' he said softly, his eyes glowing with love for his daughter. 'Your bed's been creaking all night while you tossed and turned.'

Recalling Bob Harker's lips so close to hers, hot colour flooded her face. Jess was thankful for the shadows that the flickering lamplight created to hide in.

'Bad dreams, Jess?'

'No, Pa. Just restless.'

Art Blossom fixed her with a stare: the kind of stare that could see into her heart and mind the way it always could since she'd been a nipper.

'Harker or Collins? Which were you dreaming about, Jess?'

'Bob Harker,' Jess said with a sigh, and then frustratedly wailed: 'Is it possible to fall in love with a man you've just met and know nothing about, Pa?'

Art Blossom smiled softly, his eyes reflecting his fond memories.

'If a man can fall head over heels like

I did for your mother, rest her soul, the second I set eyes on her, then I guess the same thing can happen to a woman, Jess.'

'You miss Ma terribly, don't you, Pa,' Jess said softly.

'The hurt gets worse every minute of every day, Jess,' he confessed. He sat on a chair alongside her. 'And I've got no right to ask you to marry the man I'd have you marry, Jess.' He laughed sadly. 'If my pa had forbidden me marrying your ma, I'd have upped and walked out and done it anyway. If you still want to marry Butch Collins, then you have my blessing.'

'Oh, Pa.' Jess squealed delightedly and hugged him. Then, a moment later and sobered, she asked, 'And if it's Bob Harker I want to marry?'

After a lengthy consideration of Jess's question, during which her heart beat faster and faster, Art Blossom said:

'If he loves you Jess, as much as I'm beginning to suspect you love him, he'll hang up his gun and change his ways, I reckon.'

His mood became sombre.

'Is that the way you're figuring, Jess?' he asked quietly. 'Marrying Harker?'

Now it was Jess Blossom's turn for lengthy consideration.

'Just let's say that Butch Collins doesn't seem to be the man he was only yesterday, Pa,' she concluded at last.

★　★　★

When a rider sprang from the shadows at the side of the trail Stan Baker cursed his carelessness in not having paid more attention. And though the rider was as yet unrecognizable, the Broken Arrow hardcase instinctively knew the identity of the man blocking his path.

Bart Rattigan, damn him to hell!

Maybe he could take him. It was about time that the Hett's Landing thorn in his side met his Maker.

14

'We'll stay close by, Lar,' Jeb Lacey promised Bob Harker when he was leaving his and Ned Benton's company.

'That's real good to know, Jeb,' Harker said.

'I figure that this powder-keg valley is about to blow,' was Ned Benton's opinion an opinion shared by Harker.

'Any day now, I reckon, Ned.'

'You'll be right in the thick of it, Lar,' Lacey worried. 'So as soon as you get the evidence you need, you quit the Broken Arrow, pronto.'

'Did you fellas see any illegal activity on the Bateman range?'

Both men shook their heads.

'There's every sign that Jack Bateman is coming to the end of his tether,' Benton said. 'It's impossible to say what Frank Bateman is thinking.'

'I figure that it's Jack Bateman, and

what he might do, that should concern us,' Harker said.

'Like Ned said, Jack Bateman won't stand still much longer for Collins's antics,' Lacey said. 'And it sure would be a pity if he reacts to Broken Arrow prodding, because he seems to be the kind of man who'll be needed in the valley, once Collins has been snared.'

'Well, I hope that before that happens I'll have done just that.' He was mounted, when he said as casually as he could manage: 'You know, I think it would be a good idea for you fellas to find another hidy-hole.'

'Why?' Benton quizzed.

Harker shrugged. 'Moving about the valley will reduce the risk of detection, I reckon.'

'He's right,' was Lacey's opinion. 'We'll find another place, Lar.'

Bob Harker was relieved.

'There's a gnarled old tree about a mile south of the Broken Arrow ranch house, nestling in the shelter of a ridge. There's a hole in it at its base. Leave a note there for me, telling me where your new hideout is.'

'Will do, Lar,' Jeb Lacey agreed.

Harker rode away from the shack full of troubled thoughts, and strange ones too, in which Jess Blossom loomed large. How he wished that he could ride into Hett's Landing right now, hammer on her door, and tell her that he was not the toe-rag she despised. And he found himself wishing that he would have the Sweetwater Valley mess cleared up before she tied the knot with Butch Collins, to show her the kind of man Collins really was: a man who would make her life miserable. And if he did not have Collins behind bars before Jess married him, he would have the onerous task of probably making Jess a widow, when the murderous rancher faced the hangman for his crimes.

Of course, if Frank Bateman remembered who he was, and that he had left the Pinkerton Detective Agency to become one of the governor's élite agents, he'd probably squawk and Jess would see him for what he was, a spy in her future husband's house. And should that happen, there was no way to forsee her reaction to that turn of events.

However, before Bateman should have recalled, Harker figured that whoever had followed him to the shack would blow the whistle on him with Butch Collins. In fact, he would have to be mighty careful when he returned to the Broken Arrow, and be ready at a split-second's notice to react to events that at this juncture he could not plan for.

'Damn and tarnation!' he swore. 'All of this, just when I met the woman I've been looking for all my life!'

* * *

Stan Baker's urge to draw on Rattigan was stayed by the glint of moonlight on the barrel of the sixgun the Hett's Landing lawman was holding; probably cocked, Baker reckoned.

'Twitch and I'll blast you out of the

saddle, Baker,' Rattigan warned.

'Whatever you say, Sheriff,' Baker replied genially. 'But I say that it's pretty out of order to be threatening a man out for a ride before turning in.'

'For a man who couldn't sleep, you're sure in a hurry to get to bed,' Rattigan observed drily.

'The night air's made me sleepy, I guess.' Baker's tone was mocking.

'A bullet from this .45 will surely give you the longest sleep you've ever had, Baker,' the Hett's Landing sheriff snarled. 'So don't put temptation in my way by any shenanigans. Turn and head for town.'

'Town?' Baker yelped. 'Now why would I want to go to town, Sheriff?'

'Because that's where the jail is, Baker.'

'You're throwing me in jail? What for?'

'Well for a start, for not clearing out of the territory when I told you to. And I'm sure that once I lift that rock you've crawled out from under, there'll be a whole lot of dirt to keep you in jail for a long time. That is, provided you don't swing from a gallows. Now get going!'

Baker swung his horse.

'It's a long way to town, Sheriff,' he threatened. 'You could have a real bad accident.'

15

Bob Harker's approach to the environs of the Broken Arrow was one of caution. It seemed to have the stillness about it appropriate to the early to bed early to rise of a midweek night, but the absolute stillness could also be one of ambush.

Reaching the yard without a sign of trouble, Harker led his horse to the stable. The ranch house was in darkness, as was the bunkhouse. So the question uppermost in Harker's mind was, why had his tracker not reported back to Collins? Because he reckoned that the man who had so expertly followed him got his dollars from the Broken Arrow. There might be another possibility, and that was that it was a Bateman man who had tracked him. It was possible that, curious, Frank Bateman had had him followed. But he

169

did not lend much credence to this idea, because he figured that the Big B would not have the kind of man who could track like an Indian, and move over the difficult terrain of the hill trail in the ghostly fashion of his tracker. Such a man would be of a special kind; a man who of necessity had learned to travel stealthily, probably to avoid detection by a lawman, or to creep up on an opponent or innocent he might want to waylay. Stan Baker and Bengy Smallwood came readily to mind as men who would be so skilled, having spent a great part of their life practising the art of skulking in shadows.

Leaving the stables to make his way to the bunkhouse, Bob Harker remained at a loss as to why there had not been a reception committee waiting for him. No doubt the answer would come in time, and all he could hope for was that it would not spring up and catch him unprepared.

★　★　★

Jess and Art Blossom's conversation was interrupted by a commotion in the street. Blossom went to the parlour window and raised it to look out. He saw the sheriff and another man whom he knew by sight but not by name, come along the street. The gun that Bart Rattigan was toting made it obvious that the man in front of him was not a friend. Alerted by a shout from a man having a smoke on the saloon porch, men were piling out of the Dancing Lady. Jess crowded the window alongside her pa.

'Isn't that fella Rattigan's got nailed a Broken Arrow hireling?' Blossom enquired of Jess.

'Yes,' Jess confirmed. 'That's Stan Baker.'

'I've seen him round town. Well, mostly round the saloon,' he amended critically. 'Seems to me that he's more than just a ranch hand, Jess. A gun settles too snugly on his hip for a cowhand.'

Art Blossom's shrewd assessment of Stan Baker's true value to Butch Collins resurrected the unease that Jess had been stifling for the last couple of months with a litany of excuses and a great dollop of self-deception, as Butch Collins hired more and more unlikely ranch hands.

Jess was at last forced to confront the truth about Butch Collins's intention of claiming more than his fair share of Sweetwater Valley; and claiming it in as ruthless a fashion as the hiring of such gun talent indicated. In that moment of revelation it also became clear to Jess that the real Butch Collins, hidden behind the front he showed to her, was not the man with whom she would want to spend her life.

'Pa, I'm not going to marry Butch Collins,' she declared uneqivocally.

'Spike,' Baker called out, as Rattigan shoved him towards the jail.

'Yeah, Stan,' a gangly smoker on the saloon porch called back.

'Ride out to the Broken Arrow. Tell Mr Collins what's happened.'

'Right this minute,' Spike said, swinging into the saddle.

'And tell Mr Collins that I've got real interesting news for him,' Baker added. 'Tell him that I've seen the dead walk.'

'Huh?' Spike asked, puzzled.

'Just tell him, Spike,' Baker ordered cantankerously.

'Sure will, Stan,' Spike said, galloping out of town.

As Bart Rattigan slammed the cell door on Baker the hardcase warned:

'You'll never hold me, Rattigan. You've brought a whole pile of trouble on your head.'

'If Collins tries to bust you out, Baker, my first bullet will be for you,' Rattigan promised. He strolled to his desk and sat down. 'So you'd better pray that Collins won't try.'

The sheen of sweat that broke on Baker's face pleased Bart Rattigan no end.

* * *

'There's a whole lot of trouble brewing, Jess,' Art Blossom said, closing the parlour window. 'Maybe you should go and stay with the Widow Blanch over at Owl Creek until it's settled one way or another. She'd be mighty welcoming,' he assured her.

Mention of the Widow Blanch brought to Jess's mind Henrietta Blanch's more and more frequent visits to the store, often for items that she could have included in her once-a-month shopping trip. And it was only now that she understood fully her pa's insistence on attending to the Widow Blanch's needs personally. Her pa was not a man who was easy in female company; on reflection, Jess could now see his complete lack of unease in Henrietta Blanch's presence.

'Pa?'

Art Blossom saw the light of recognition in his daughter's gaze.

'Don't you go getting ideas, gal. The widow and me are just good friends,' he hurriedly reassured Jess. Too hurriedly and too stridently, perhaps. 'No one will ever take the place of your ma.'

'That goes without saying, Pa,' Jess said. 'But if I get married, it won't be good for you to be alone. And I reckon that Henrietta Blanch would be very convivial company of an evening.'

'You talk real nonsense now and then, Jess!' Then, startled: 'You said you weren't marrying Butch Collins.'

'Who said anything about Butch Collins, Pa.'

'Harker?'

Jess sighed in the dangerously dreamy way that in Art Blossom's experience, a woman in love did.

'Maybe,' Jess sighed.

With a sinking heart, Art Blossom reckoned that there was no maybe about it. And all he could hope for was that Harker would say no.

★ ★ ★

Frank Bateman woke suddenly from a restless sleep. 'Lar Blaney!' he exclaimed. 'That's who Harker is!'

16

Finding sleep impossible, Bob Harker had lain on his bunk fully clothed, and was wide awake to hear the thunder of hoofs arriving in the yard and the rider's yell of alarm to the ranch house.

'Rattigan's slung Stan Baker in jail, Mr Collins!'

Men were leaping from their bunks and crowding the bunkhouse door. Spike repeated his message to them, unnecessarily so, because their presence in the small hours should have told him that they had already heard.

Lamps were being lit in the house, and moments later a sour-faced Butch Collins appeared at the front door, his earlier bout of whiskey-slugging show-ing in his bloodshot eyes and craggy face.

'I heard, Lowry,' he growled, when

Spike began to relay the by now familar message.

'Stan says he's got interestin' news, Mr Collins,' Spike Lowry announced.

Harker, who had remained on his bunk fully clothed, slid from under the blankets and buckled on his gunbelt.

'News?' Collins was brushing away his whiskey cobwebs. 'What kind of interesting news would that be?'

'Stan didn't say, Mr Collins. I guess he'll tell you when you get to town.' Frowning, uncertain about relaying the rest of what Baker had told him to tell Collins, he mumbled: 'Stan said . . . '

'Said what?' Collins growled impatiently.

'That he's seen the dead walk, Mr Collins.'

Bob Harker settled the .45 on his right hip, fully expecting now to have to use it shortly. And knowing that, out-numbered as he was, his would be a fight that could not be won.

'Baker's seen the dead walk?' Collins checked, shaking his head as if to regroup his whiskey-scattered wits.

'Makes no sense to me neither,' was Spike Lowry's conclusion. 'But that's what Stan said to tell ya, Mr Collins.'

Although Stan Baker's message made no sense to Butch Collins presently, Harker estimated that his confusion would not last for long. But maybe it would last long enough for him to leave and reorganize. He knew that from now on, with his original plan in tatters, he would be hostage to circumstance, forced to react when he would prefer to initiate.

But the final hand had been dealt, and he would have to play the cards dealt him.

'Want us to saddle up, Mr Collins?'

Harker recognized Bengy Smallwood's voice.

'No,' was Collins's decision. 'First light will do.'

'But Stan's languishing in jail, Mr Collins,' Smallwood said, obviously a tad annoyed that Collins was willing to long-finger his partner's discomfort.

'First light, I said,' Butch Collins barked.

Harker heard the solid slam of the ranch house door.

'It ain't right that Stan's got to — '

'Then you go and do somethin' 'bout it, if you want, Smallwood,' a man in the crowd clogging up the bunkhouse door said sourly.

'I might just do that, Sullivan,' Smallwood replied angrily.

'Yeah, in a pig's eye,' another man mocked.

'You'll see,' Smallwood barked. The man's low opinion of Smallwood's solo commitment was proved right, when Smallwood said: 'Well, after all, Mr Collins is the boss.'

Smallwood joined the rest of the men filing back into the bunkhouse. Harker dived back under the blankets. If they saw him fully clothed and wearing a gun, it would start all sorts of questions that he had no answers to, and he had not the time to think up believable untruths.

He waited until the sound of snoring rattled the rafters before he again slid from under the blankets. He made his way quickly to the stables and saddled his horse who, having her rest cut short, was fidgety.

'Easy, girl,' he coaxed the crotchety mare. 'I hate interfering with your sleep, but hanging around here isn't very healthy right now.'

'You got that right, Harker!' The governor's agent froze. He turned slowly to meet Bengy Smallwood, who was cock-a-hoop. 'Me and Stan always figgered there was something not right 'bout you. So, not seeing you take any interest in Spike Lowry's arrival, I had a feeling that you were more interested in something else. Yourself! Then, when I went back into the bunkhouse I saw something that was real interesting. There was no boots under your bunk, Harker. Now I asked m'self, why would a man go to bed with his boots on?'

He chuckled meanly. ''Cause he

wanted to be ready to get up again, pronto.'

'Clever fella, Smallwood,' Harker said, kicking himself that he had equated lowbrow outlaw behaviour with dumbness.

'Can't say the same 'bout you,' Smallwood crowed. 'Now, unbuckle your gunbelt and sling it over here. Then we'll go and see Mr Collins.' His chuckle became meaner still. 'You know, I figure that you'll be strung up after all, Mr high-and-mighty lawman. 'Cause that's what I figger you are, Harker. The gunbelt,' he snarled.

Harker thought about drawing, but saw no prospect of winning, seeing that Smallwood was already toting a cocked sixgun. So without another option open to him, he had to comply with the hardcase's demand.

Looking failure in the face and embittered that his grand scheme to nail Butch Collins for his crimes had gone up in smoke, he unbuckled his gunbelt and slung it to Smallwood.

'Sling me that lariat from your saddle too,' Smallwood instructed. 'Might as well come prepared with the necessary for Collins to hang you.' The rope in his possession, the hardcase went on: 'Now, let's mosey over to the house.'

Crossing the yard to the ranch house, Harker reckoned that he was counting down the minutes to the end of his mission, and the end of his life, too.

★ ★ ★

Stan Baker was pacing his cell, his agitation getting more frantic by the minute.

'Looks like Butch Collins ain't in a hurry to spring you from jail, Baker,' Bart Rattigan said. 'Might just let you rot here.'

'He'll come,' Baker said, but sounding none too sure that the rancher would.

A couple of minutes later, hearing hoofs on the street outside, Rattigan got up and went to the window.

'Told you so,' Baker crowed.

The Hett's Landing sheriff chuckled.

'What're you laughing at, Rattigan?' Baker demanded to know.

'It's only Spike Lowry arriving back, Baker. Alone,' he added pointedly.

The outlaw's jaw dropped.

'Get him in here,' he shouted despairingly.

Bart Rattigan glanced back out through the law office window.

'I don't reckon he'd like that,' he opined. 'Not the way Lowry is giving the jail as wide a berth as the street will permit.'

'Ah, let him be,' Baker said in a swaggering fashion. 'Mr Collins is on his way.'

'Yeah,' Rattigan said, with a mocking sneer. 'I figure that if that was so, Spike Lowry would be beating down my door to tell you, Baker.'

Stan Baker resumed his pacing, sensing the cell closing in on him. So much so that Bart Rattigan figured that soon his prisoner would be climbing the bars.

★　★　★

Bob Harker was thinking faster than a rattler's spit. He glanced over his shoulder to gauge how close Smallwood was. Not close enough, he concluded. And the hardcase exercised caution by dropping back further, anticipating a move by the governor's agent.

'I'm right behind you, Harker,' he barked. 'So don't get no smart ideas. You'll be dead before you move.'

Every second Harker was getting nearer the house and his demise. He feigned a stumble, hoping that the gap between Smallwood and himself would shorten before the outlaw could realize that it had. His ruse worked exactly as he hoped it would. The seconds Smallwood lost in trying to figure out whether Harker had genuinely stumbled or whether his lurch forward was trickery was all Harker needed to round on him, his boot flying through the air to connect with Smallwood's kneecap. The hardcase howled and his left leg buckled,

throwing him off balance. Harker lost
no time in swinging a pile-driver to the
side of Smallwood's head that sent him
reeling. He followed through with a gut-
busting hammer-blow to the belly. A
gush of rancid air from Smallwood's
wide-open mouth washed over Harker.
He delivered a blow to Smallwood's
ribcage. A sickening snap of bone made
Harker's skin crawl. Incredibly, Smallwood still held on to his pistol, and even
more incredibly he managed to swing it
towards Harker who had to grapple for
the Colt in a deadly struggle, all the
time conscious of the company that must
appear presently from the bunkhouse
on hearing the ruckus in the yard. Fitter
than his opponent, Harker turned the
gun into the outlaw's belly and pulled
the trigger. The belly-flesh soaked up
the gun's explosion but not completely.
A light flared in the bunkhouse. Harker
fled to his horse which had wandered
out of the stable, the mare following her
natural instincts when saddled. Smallwood lay writhing on the ground, his

moans getting weaker by the second as his life ebbed away. Harker thundered out of the yard just as the bunkhouse door and the ranch house door were flung open. Collins was the quickest to react, and laid lead after Harker for the half-minute it took the law agent to round the side of the house.

'Mount up!' Collins roared.

As he galloped out across the range, Bob Harker wished that his horse had had more rest. Though he had a good lead, he knew that the fresher mounts of the Broken Arrow pursuers would quickly close the distance between them. And once they caught up with him, he would be certain to meet the fate from which Bart Rattigan had saved him.

It looked like his escape from a lynch rope had been only a temporary reprieve.

Looking behind him only minutes after his escape, Harker saw the band of riders, some still in long johns, in hectic pursuit led by Butch Collins. They were men used to saddling up, and had not lost any time. Harker had been thinking about trying to beat them to town where, now that his plans had gone awry, he intended to enlist Bart Rattigan's help by revealing who he was. But it would be unfair to visit his troubles on the Hett's Landing lawman now, when he had not taken him into his confidence to begin with. Besides, with Butch Collins in the ugly mood he was in, Harker doubted if a mere sheriff's badge would prevent him from taking his revenge. And if Rattigan stood in the way, he'd probably never see the pension he was so looking forward to collecting.

That left only one alternative that he could see. He would have to seek refuge with Frank Bateman. The Big B was nearer than town, but with his horse flagging fast, even the lesser distance might prove too much for the mare.

17

In the Hett's Landing jail, Stan Baker's initial certainty that Butch Collins would rescue him from Bart Rattigan's clutches was slipping away by the minute, and he faced the prospect of Rattigan shipping him out to the territorial capital to face the justice his foul deeds merited — a gallows. In his panic the seed of an idea was taking root. What if he could strike a deal with the sheriff? And, more important, with Harker? who he now suspected was a governor's agent, to chronicle Butch Collins's litany of murder and treachery. Thinking so, Baker saw a light at the end of a very dark tunnel. If Collins had abandoned him, then damn him to hell. He was, if at all possible, going to save his neck.

'Sheriff,' he summoned.

Dozing, Bart Rattigan shifted grumpily

in his chair and, deciding to ignore his prisoner, began to doze again.

'Sheriff,' Baker barked. 'I'm ready to talk plenty about Butch Collins's antics.'

On hearing the hardcase's startling statement, Rattigan forgot about sleep.

'Is that a fact, Baker?'

'It is. I was right alongside him when he shot Frank Bateman in the back. And also when he murdered those who got in his way.'

'Alongside him?' Rattigan questioned.

Baker snorted. 'Which means, Rattigan, that if you want me to talk, you'll have to forget that I was.'

The Hett's Landing sheriff shrugged.

'That's a decision that a higher authority than me would have to make, Baker. Because I reckon that you're wanted in most territories.'

'I ride free, or there's no deal!' Baker stated uncompromisingly.

'You're not exactly in a position to bargain,' Rattigan reminded his prisoner. 'It was my intention to ship you off to the territorial capital.'

'I figured as much,' Baker said. 'But I was thinking more of crossing the border to Mexico and heading to the South Americas.'

'Why the change of heart?' Rattigan wanted to know.

'Well, it looks like *Mr* high-and-mighty Collins intends to let me keep that date with the hangman that I should have kept a long time ago, if truth be known. So I figured that I'd switch places with him by giving the low-down on the bastard to the law.'

Bart Rattigan laughed.

'Rats turning on each other. Mighty pleasing, I'd say.'

'Do we have a deal?' Baker growled.

'I'll telegraph the governor's office. See if the governor will bite.'

'I reckon that a deal can be struck right here in Hett's Landing, Sheriff.' The positive nature of Baker's statement got Rattigan's undivided attention. 'I figure that there's a governor's special agent right here.'

The hardcase chuckled at Bart

Rattigan's surprise. 'In fact, I reckon there's three special agents on your doorstep, Rattigan.'

Stan Baker went on to chronicle what he had witnessed at the shack in the hills.

'I'll be damned,' Rattigan swore, on hearing about Jeb Lacey's resurrection. 'Smart fella, Harker.'

'That ain't his real name either,' Baker said. 'The walking dead man called him Lar.'

Rattigan slapped his knee.

'Ain't you a bundle of surprises, Baker!'

The sound of a rider got Rattigan's attention. And when boots sounded on the boardwalk outside the sheriff's office, he was out of his chair and behind the door toting a rifle in seconds. Stan Baker had a new worry. What if Collins had decided to spring him? He had been ready to squeal. And he had no doubt that Bart Rattigan would use his betrayal to put a wedge between him and Collins; a wedge that would see him hanging from the first tree that Butch Collins came to. Or hot lead in the gut.

Bart Rattigan tensed, ready to deliver a swift blow or an equally swift bullet if the nocturnal caller offered a threat. Baker, weak with fright, sought what little shadow his cell offered.

The door of the sheriff's office began to open.

★   ★   ★

The gap between the Broken Arrow riders and Bob Harker was closing fast. Not as knowledgeable as he would like to be in the terrain, he hoped that he was shortening and not lengthening the distance to the Big B. He was also only too aware that the three riders who had branched off from the main bunch not long before might very well be planning to cut him off.

Harker urged the mare on, but despite his coaxing and cajoling the horse slowed, and was close to being completely winded. Up ahead there was a stretch of wooded trail — a good ambush location. He faced a stark choice. Risk the wooded stretch of trail ahead. Or veer off in another direction. His problem was, that should he veer off what he reckoned was the established route to the Bateman ranch he might be heading into more trouble rather than avoiding it.

★ ★ ★

Jack Bateman strode into the Hett's Landing sheriff's office, and sprang back from Bart Rattigan's cocked rifle pointing squarely at him.

'That was a damn fool thing to do at dead of night, Jack!' a much relieved Rattigan rebuked Frank Bateman's nephew. 'Why the hell didn't you call out, man?'

Recognizing the validity of the sheriff's rebuke, Jack Bateman apologized.

'Sorry, Bart.' His gaze went to Stan

Baker. 'I would have, if I'd realized that you had a snake in here.'

'What're you doing in town at this hour?' Rattigan quizzed the rancher's nephew.

'My uncle sent me to tell you that he remembers who Harker is, and Harker ain't his real name. He's an *hombre* called Lar Blaney. And he's a — '

'Governor's special agent?'

Bateman was taken aback. 'How do you know that, Bart?'

'Baker tracked Harker to a shack in the hills where he met two other men, one a dead man.'

'Huh?' Jack Bateman grunted, astonished. 'And why would Baker tell you what he saw and heard, Bart?'

'Simple. He wants to save his neck. Says that he'll spill the beans on Butch Collins, if he's let ride across the border in return for his evidence.'

Jack Bateman laughed.

'Like I said, Bart, I'd surely have called out if I knew there was a snake in here.'

★　★　★

Faced with two options that could prove equally deadly, Bob Harker chose to stick to the well-worn trail to the Big B. He rode into the wooded stretch, his every muscle tensed, expecting at any second to feel the burn of a bullet.

★　★　★

Jeb Lacey and Ned Benton, worried about the pit of danger into which their fellow agent could drop once he returned to the Broken Arrow, had wisely decided to follow along. They had almost intervened when Bengy Smallwood had marched Harker across the yard to the Collins ranch house, but Benton had sagely decided that Harker would outwit his captor. Now, as they saw the three riders break away from the main Broken Arrow bunch, they were glad that they had kept their powder dry. Having scouted the valley in their reconnoitring activities, Lacey and Benton's knowledge of it was much superior to Harker's, and they reckoned that the separating riders were circling round Harker to get ahead of him to the wooded stretch of trail that the agent would pass through. Having the edge on the breaking riders, they had gambled on their assumption being correct. Now, as they watched the three Broken Arrow riders settle down to await Harker's arrival, the duo knew that they had chosen wisely.

'He's comin',' one of the men, the furthest forward, called in a hoarse whisper.

Jeb Lacey stepped out from the shadows to confront him, sixgun cocked; the man yelped and staggered backwards.

'Stay away from me,' he whined, and screamed, 'You're dead!'

A second man, equally scared, tumbled down the wooded slope in his efforts to escape from what he thought was a ghostly apparition. The third of the trio, made of sterner stuff, went for his gun. Ned Benton reared up from the shadows behind him to clip him on the head.

For the brief moment before Lacey and Benton hailed him, Bob Harker was at a loss when he saw two running men constantly glancing behind. They fled past Harker, wide-eyed, muttering about having seeing a ghost.

The agents permitted themselves a brief humorous interlude before Harker explained where he was headed, and his connection with Frank Bateman.

'Bateman will have the men to make a fair fight of this,' he said.

'You make tracks for the Big B, Lar,' Lacey said. 'We'll hold out here for as long as we can.'

'But not for too long,' Harker cautioned. 'No heroics. Fade away while you still have the chance.'

An agreement to that effect copper-fastened, Harker changed mounts with Jeb Lacey. With a fresh horse he lost no time in covering the remaining ground to the Big B. He thundered into the Bateman yard, leapt from his saddle and ran with his horse.

Two men barred his way to the ranch house, until an upstairs window was lifted and Frank Bateman ordered:

'Let him into the house.'

'Are you sure about that, Mr Bateman?' one of the men checked.

'I'm sure, Clark,' the rancher barked back.

The men stepped aside, puzzled by Bateman's open-house policy towards the Broken Arrow's new fast gun. When Harker got inside, Bateman was wheeling himself to the top of the stairs.

'Up here, Lar,' he said.

'So you remembered,' Harker said with a chuckle. 'I figured you would, Frank.'

'Trouble?' Bateman quizzed him as he mounted the stairs.

'Trouble,' Harker confirmed.

'Broken Arrow trouble?'

Harker nodded. 'About twenty men on my tail.'

'Clark!' Frank Bateman hollered. The front door opened instantly and a man's head popped in. 'Rouse the men. There's fighting to be done.'

'With the Broken Arrow?' he asked eagerly.

'Yes,' Bateman confirmed.

Clark hurried away, hollering at the top of his lungs.

'I'm sorry that I'm dumping this mess on your doorstep, Frank,' Harker apologized.

'It would have come sooner or later,' the Big B owner growled. 'And now that it's come, let it be settled one way or another!'

★   ★   ★

'I'm willing to talk, are you willing to listen, Rattigan?' Stan Baker asked, anxious to be out of jail and on the trail to the border as fast as he could.

'You talk, Baker. I'll get pencil and paper and write it all down. Then you can sign it.'

'Not so fast, Rattigan,' the hardcase growled. 'I don't sign until I'm mounted and ready to ride. Deal?'

'Deal,' Rattigan agreed.

Twenty minutes later, Rattigan put down his pencil, pleased as a cat after a saucer of fresh milk. Reading through Baker's statement, he concluded:

'This is enough to hang Butch Collins ten times over.'

'Now ain't you glad that I didn't leave the territory when you told me to, Sheriff,' Stan Baker crowed.

★　★　★

'Get me a rifle and push me over to the window, Lar,' Bateman ordered Blaney. 'Heck, I ain't going to miss a second of this lead-slinging shindig.'

'I want Collins alive,' Blaney said.

'Only if that's possible,' Bateman returned. 'You can't expect a man to sacrifice his life in a straight shoot-out.'

'Only if it's possible,' Blaney agreed. 'It's just that I'd like Butch Collins to swing in the breeze like those nesters he lynched.'

Settled at the window, Frank Bateman delivered the agent's wishes to the men lining up to face the Broken Arrow charge, making it clear that no man was to sacrifice his life to deliver on the order.

★　★　★

'Ride through it!' Collins ordered on reaching the wooded stretch of trail where Lacey and Benton were lurking, when the men began to slow up.

'That's loco,' a man near to Collins protested.

Collins blasted the protester out of his saddle and then turned to meet any other threat, of which there was none.

'Ride,' he barked. 'Right to the front door of the Big B, where I reckon Harker's sought refuge.' He sat ramrod-straight in the saddle, his scowl as evil as Satan's. 'Let's make this valley

Broken Arrow range for once and for all!'

Jeb Lacey and Ned Benton laid as much lead as they could on the Broken Arrow crew, but fast-galloping targets being difficult to nail, all except three of the riders made it through before they did as agreed with Harker and vanished into the trees, from where they made their way to the Big B behind the Collins bunch.

'Riders!' the Big B look-out hollered, as the Collins outfit swarmed out of the dark.

Guns started blasting, lead flying to and fro. The air filled with the screams of men as they were downed. Some of the cries were short, others dragged on. Dead and wounded.

The fight was furious but short-lived, a lot of the Broken Arrow men, unwilling to throw away their lives in the headlong charge Butch Collins wanted, turned tail. With the number of fighting men dwindling, Collins decided to quit also. Lar Blaney spotted the rancher slinking into the night. He risked the buzzing lead and ran to his horse. Mounted, he galloped after Collins, shouting:

'Collins is running out!'

The Broken Arrow gunfire fizzled out.

'There's nowhere to run to, Collins,' Blaney growled grimly. 'Time to pay the piper!'

Now their positions were reversed. Blaney was on a loose-limbed, fast moving stallion, while Butch Collins's horse was nearly spent. The chase was a brief one. Drawing level with the rancher, Blaney leaped on his back and dragged him from the saddle. They crashed heavily to the ground, but grim determination brought Blaney to his feet first. And just as Collins was struggling to regain his wind, he landed the pile-driver of all pile-drivers on the side of the rancher's head. Butch Collins hit the ground with the force of a boulder dropped from a thousand feet.

Bart Rattigan looked up when Lar Blaney shoved Collins ahead of him into the sheriff's office.

'Jail him!' he ordered, and flashed the gold badge of a governor's special agent, 'while I gather the evidence to hang him. I'm sorry, but I couldn't risk confiding in you, Sheriff,' he apologized. 'You could have been on Collins's payroll.'

'For even thinking that, I want to meet you behind the livery when this whole rotten episode is over and done with. I'm going to beat the hell out of you,' the Hett's Landing lawman promised.

'That seems fair to me,' Blaney agreed.

Bart Rattigan fluttered Stan Baker's statement in front of him before handing it over to Blaney, who read it with a startled gaze. He looked to the cells.

'Where's Baker now?'

'Headed for the border.'

Rattigan explained the details of his agreement with the outlaw.

'He's not going to make it!' Blaney declared, heading for the door.

★ ★ ★

A week later Lar Blaney arrived back in Hett's Landing with Baker in tow, and when he'd slung him in Rattigan's jail he kept a date with Bart Rattigan behind the livery. The fight lasted almost fifteen minutes, and Jess Blossom suffered through every second of it, until both men were standing on legs that wobbled. Bruised and battered they hung on to each other.

'Had enough, Rattigan?' Blaney enquired, gasping.

'No!' Rattigan growled between lips that were ten times their normal size. 'You?'

'No,' Blaney said, his jaw lopsided.

'Well, I have!' Jess Blossom strode into the clearing to berate both men. 'You two, as lawmen, are suppose to give good example to other citizens, not beat each other senseless. You're coming with me.'

Jess offered an arm to each man.

'Grab hold,' she ordered. 'Before you fall flat on your faces.' Striding ahead, with Bart Rattigan and Lar Blaney painfully trying to keep pace, she scolded: 'You two are a pretty sight for sure.'

'Best delay the wedding for a couple of weeks, Jess,' Rattigan said. 'You wouldn't want to walk down the aisle with a man looking like a mule's rear end, now would you?'

Jess Blossom blushed and flustered:

'Wedding? What in tarnation are you talking about, Bart Rattigan?'

'Ah, heck, don't pretend that you're not going to tame Lar,' the sheriff chuckled, grimacing painfully. And looking at Blaney, he continued: 'And don't you give me any guff either about not knowing what I'm talking about. All I ask is that you name the first boy Bart.'

Blaney laughed as best he could with a lopsided jaw.

'Rattigan, you sure do have some grand and fine ideas from time to time.' He smiled at Jess. 'I know it isn't the right time to ask, Jess. But — '

'I will!'

'Yeah,' Lar Blaney exclaimed, and added: 'Yeeeahah!'

Bart Rattigan took the sheriff's badge from his shirt and pinned it on Blaney.

'You'll be needing a steady job near your wife and family from now on, instead of gadflying about the territory as one of those fancy governor's agents. I'll whittle away my time to pension as your deputy, if that's OK with you, Sheriff Blaney?'

'I'd deem that a great honour, Bart,' Blaney said.

'Ain't going to do much,' Rattigan warned.

'Not going to ask you to,' Lar Blaney assured his new deputy.

★   ★   ★

The following day, as Butch Collins and Stan Baker were being escorted to the stage bound for the territorial capital, where they would stand trial for murder, a wagon arriving in town was spooked by a barking stray dog and took fright and mowed down Collins. Jess Blossom had a pang of sadness, but she reckoned that Butch Collins's demise under the wheels of a charging wagon was better than him climbing the gallows that was inevitably awaiting him.

⋆   ⋆   ⋆

A month later, a notice was pinned to the door of the general store. It read:

Closed for a wedding.
Business as usual tomorrow.
Signed: Art Blossom.

There was a second notice on the law office door.

The same applies here as at the General Store.
Signed: Sheriff Lar Blaney.

We do hope that you have enjoyed reading this large print book.

Did you know that all of our titles are available for purchase?

We publish a wide range of high quality large print books including:
Romances, Mysteries, Classics General Fiction Non Fiction and Westerns

Special interest titles available in large print are:
The Little Oxford Dictionary Music Book, Song Book Hymn Book, Service Book

Also available from us courtesy of Oxford University Press:
Young Readers' Dictionary (large print edition) Young Readers' Thesaurus (large print edition)

For further information or a free brochure, please contact us at:
**Ulverscroft Large Print Books Ltd., The Green, Bradgate Road, Anstey, Leicester, LE7 7FU, England.
Tel:** (00 44) 0116 236 4325
Fax: (00 44) 0116 234 0205

I

PONDERFOOT'S DOLLARS

Ben Coady

Already under the threat of losing his farm and being shunned by the community, Jack Barley faces his biggest problem yet. The notorious Bannion brothers arrive to rob the local bank, tracked by a deadly US Marshal. To avoid danger, they hit on a scheme involving Jack: in return for his wife and son's safety, he must rob the bank ... Jack complies with their demands, but the marshal is suspicious and the money is missing — can he save his family?